The Glassman

MultiMind

First paperback edition, September 2023
First e-book edition, September 2023

Cover art by Ejiwa Ebenebe
Edited by Ja'el Knotts

ISBN 978-1-952860-10-2 (paperback)
ISBN 978-1-952860-11-9 (ebook)
ISBN 978-1-952860-12-6 (audiobook)

Library of Congress Control Number: 2022908004

www.multimindpublishing.com

Acknowledgment

To my favorite band – hopefully this doesn't make things weird.

This book is partially funded by the Maryland State Arts Council creativity grant.

A special thank you to Lisa Marbel, thank you for being so kind.

Perry, I wish you got to read the whole book before you passed – but I am glad you liked the beginning.

<u>Content Warning:</u>

- Depression/Trauma
- Suicidal Ideation/Self-Harm

THE GLASSMAN

Part One: The Existence

In a future not far from our present day, things have changed. Summers are hotter. Days are hazier in the city of San Diego. In the home of Jacob "Mars" Juarez, the morning light rose away from his bedroom window as the sun further ascended, waking him no earlier than anyone else naturally would on his street.

He opened his brown eyes, the open windows stood before him as the waft of the waking city ebbed through the gathered lace of the copper curtains. The curtains swayed lazily at the gathers in the soft wind on that gentle humid day. His eyes then fell upon the curly, russet hair of his wife, Danielle Juarez. The white cover had drifted from her bare, dark gold shoulder in the night. The strap of her black tank top nestled against her neck as she slumbered. From the feel of the room and how tucked her head was in the pillow, he surmised she cried herself to sleep for another night that week.

Mars lifted the covers slightly to check for any abrasions or cuts he may have caused her or any possible evidence left between them. Nothing but the shadow of space between them. A good sign.

Danielle stirred gently and opened her auburn eyes to the chattering birds sitting outside the window, just out of view. She felt the crisp dryness of her eyes. Flashes of last night came to her, muffled sobbing resounding in her ears. She willed the sorrowful memories away and settled herself better. She could feel her husband behind her, his back against hers. Danielle closed her eyes to wait for any prick or sting to greet her. Nothing but the heat of her husband and his gaze as he turned over to her. She loved him dearly, but now she feared the morning she would wake at the pearly gates.

Mars felt a light ebb of joy deep within. For yet another night, his wife still slept beside him. That she still loved him despite his changes. Some days, he wished she would leave him and take their children, Vivica and Violet, with her to a life anew. It would pain him greatly, yes, but at least he would know that they were safe at least. Not a day went by that he didn't think of Dao, his bassist and longtime friend. Mars would never forgive himself if he did the same to his beloved family.

It was an accident! Mars quickly defended to himself. Thoughts flooded back to San Diego Rivers Memorial Hospital as he blinked away tears. *Why, why did I survive?* Just like every day, the haunting thought returned. Ever since he woke up in the hospital, such awful thoughts and wonders visited him day after day, relentless and pervasive. *I should be dead.*

Danielle turned carefully to her husband, sure to catch a piece of glass in the act, maybe. She looked at his forlorn face. The same face that still warmed her with its wonderful brown sienna chilled her to the core all the same. She smiled at him.

"Morning," she softly greeted.

Mars looked up at her. Her face always reminded him every day that perhaps life could still be worth living. He returned her smile weakly.

"Morning," he mumbled sleepily. Mars remembered how Danielle would comb her gentle fingers through his long, reddish-black dreadlocks as his eyes adored her face. What bliss seeing that face had brought him through all the eleven years they had been together. He wanted to caress her cheek but dared not to.

Reminding her arm to keep close, Danielle gazed upon Mars playfully. She asked, "How are you feeling?"

The question was like a soft blade on a vital vein, it stung Mars so. He used to hide it so well, but his cape of illusion had worn quite threadbare by now.

His eyes fell askance. "Okay, I guess," he murmured.

Danielle assured him, "'Okay' is good."

Breakfast was served and Mars prepared to go to work – or, as Mars saw it now: the worst part of the day. He wore his tahms more often now since Dao's incident. He wore a navy and black tahm today, bloated with his thick, hip-length dreads. It matched his black basketball jersey from Mindware and dark blue canvas shorts. Mars grabbed his keys off the table next to the glass-paned door as the rest of his family prepared for a new day of elementary school in the back bedroom Vivica and Violet shared. He could hear light fussing waft out the door as there was a small squabble over shoes Danielle tried to quell. Mars stopped short of placing the keys in his pocket. Mars just couldn't go. He couldn't harm another. Moving through the world felt cold and alone but, he sighed to himself: there was no other way.

Danielle came out from their daughters' bedroom to get an apple from the dining table, she needed a quick break from the early morning chaos. Instead, she found Mars standing there in front of their door, gaze tossed to the wooden floor, arms limp and keys loosely cupped in his hands. *Mars*, she thought mournfully as she started towards him, her slippered feet padding across the floor.

Hearing his name being lightly called, Mars looked up at his wife behind him. She held his hand and touched his face, forgetting her precautions. "Mars, you have to get to work, babe. You can't stay here all day." She curled his thicker hands into hers and held it to her heart. "We'll all see you tonight. Have a great day at the studio." Danielle pecked Mars on the cheek. She wished for his lips but it was too much of a risk.

Mars wanted the same. There was so much he wanted but so little he could have now. Even the grasp of a hand ached his heart, how long it had been since he had much more than that.

Danielle turned around to go back to the girls' room. She was sure there was more chaos in her absence, she could hear playing. Mars wrapped his heavily tattooed arms around her neck and waist in desperate comfort. It caught Danielle off-guard. Her face blanked with panic but Mars couldn't help but to hold her tight and mutter to her, "I'm sorry, I just really love and miss your embrace. I feel so alone. I need you." His face nestled into her shoulder and against her neck.

Danielle felt abysmal and torn. She didn't want to get nicked or worse, suffer a fatal slip – but the forced distance, it bred nothing but clanging loneliness. She relaxed herself, she tried to. Danielle missed the comforting touch of her husband. She could tell that he missed her more. His arms wrapped around her closer, tighter.

"I love you, too," she replied softly.

The moment passed, quiet and calm. Then Mars' arms started to feel … jagged.

His skin jutted and moved, as if rumbling rocks rolled underneath his tattooed skin. They sharpened and jumbled about, biting into her skin.

"Mars?" She choked as she grew into a gasping panic. Danielle tapped his arm fervently as she tried to keep her voice low so the girls wouldn't hear, "*Mars.*"

He held on, Mars couldn't bear to let go. It had been too long since he's felt her touch–

Danielle wrenched herself away from her husband. She tried to hold in her sniffles, her eyes filled with hot tears. She stared at him with the fear she hated. Again, distance was between them.

Mars' skin settled. Another surge, another day. He couldn't control them, he barely knew how. Or even if he could. The fear in her eyes stung him like ice, he turned his head away. A small surge rolled about underneath his skin in simmering spurts until they quelled into nothing.

Danielle tried to blink back the tears but more came instead. *It wasn't on purpose*, she tried to remind herself. *Mars didn't mean it. It's not his fault. Not his fault.* She knew Mars didn't ask for this, for what he changed into. But still she kicked herself: just had to slip back to normal again, that she could be comfortable again, that she could let her guard down again. Even the best days felt like the worst and she hated every minute of it. She remembered what she promised back when Mars was in the hospital, *We'll make the best of it, honey. We're all going to get through this. You, me, and the girls.* No one said this was going to be fair. Then again, almost no one knew anything about Mars' new condition.

"I'm – I'm fine," Danielle sniffed. She quickly wiped away her tears. "Hon-honestly, Mars. I'm fine." Her throat and hips still burned with the shadows of his surging touch. How sharp everything became. "It's fine. *You're* fine." She padded forward to hold his hands, just like she always would, but stopped short.

Her words rang hollow to Mars. Memories of Dao bleeding out on the studio floor flooded in. How the bassist clutched his face, how the blood smeared over everything as it dripped from his deep mahogany skin. Dao's cries of mercy and fear filled Mars' ears. Mars couldn't break from the guilt, the wild stare Dao shot him with his remaining eye wouldn't leave him. A loose thought sailed across his mind, *I did it again.* He glanced at his wife, her feigned smile and fearful eyes. *All my doing.*

Mars mumbled out a feeble apology as he clutched his keys and left. He tried not to slam the door.

A heavy jam session was underway in the decorative studio, tucked away deep in a distant corner of Mindware's storage warehouse. Mindware was a local store for skaters and trick bike riders. They were the first supporters of the band playing in their studio, Lumination Rising.

It was only the guitarist, Isaiah Corbin, and drummer, Alvin 'Amos' Zavala, also Mars' cousin. Amos and Isaiah created Lumination Rising back when they were in high school during lunch one day and stuck together since. The music that grooved in the studio was moving but with Dao out, it failed to thrive without their low-end anchor. Amos and Isaiah tried their best to make up for the absence, but it wasn't the same. No one to joke about how little energy drinks were part of the meager budget of their second proper album. No one there to show a new card trick they picked up. No silly antics, nothing. The studio had less life. The doctors said Dao would be back and playing in three more weeks, maybe a little sooner. His right eye was healing fine and he was lucky to only have a nick to his jugular instead of a whole sever but he would forever suffer blindness. Despite such news, Dao seemed to improve in spirits in each video call he had with Amos and Isaiah. Amos wanted Mars to be part of the calls but Isaiah always refused the idea, he figured it was smarter to leave Mars out. Unfortunately, Isaiah was right, Dao avoided any subject to do with Mars and the scars he would bear forever from his brow to his neck. Every time the conversation steered towards Mars, Dao would do anything to steer it away.

Mars sometimes would attend the video calls, mostly by accidentally walking in on them. Every time, Mars and Dao would exchange polite pleasantries but not much else. Mars had to work to be involved in any video conversation. Phone calls were shorter and texts sometimes went unanswered. Eventually, Mars resigned himself to ask Amos the questions and get updated that way.

Riffing his diamond blue guitar one last time, Isaiah announced over Amos' drums, "Break time!" Amos stilled his cymbals as Isaiah repeated himself, "I wanna take a break, man." He had shock silver curls, they suited his deep copper complexion, which was covered in countless tattoos.

Amos nodded, his skin a sweaty, rose-gold brown. He rubbed his face with the hem of his gray Mindware shirt. The design on the front featured an open head displaying a brain shaped together with Tetris pieces. Amos threw his sticks on the crimson towel beside his feet as he got up. This session felt more rewarding today than it had that whole week.

Isaiah took a swig of water from his dingy yellow sports bottle. Amos stretched his broad shoulders and then stepped out from behind his drum-set to stroll into the mini kitchen nestled in the corner of the crowded room. On the opposite wall stood a towering ornate mural of the Lady of Guadalupe, hand painted by one of Mindware's longest artists, a young college kid who never went anywhere without at least a king marker and a stubby can of spray paint. Amos once caught her tagging the back of his bass drum. He paid her to do the rest. Now, his studio drums were the centerpiece of the room.

The studio was a bit atypical. The walls were professionally sound-proofed but it was glaringly obvious the room used to be a lounging area. There were still couches, rugs and chairs among the mics and amps. Headphones were laid upon spent boxes of pizza and calzones. The space was put up by Mindware as a gift to the band for their successful first album, *Carnival of the Casualty.* It went gold in ten months, silver in the United Kingdom. The success was in part thanks to their tiny, local label, Delirium Shack Records. In efforts to cut creation costs and keep the money in the community, the band saw nothing but good things from this. They now had a place to practice that wouldn't dig into their pockets and a merch deal to boot from Mindware, giving them clothes to wear and sell. As far as bands not on major labels go, Lumination Rising had struck lucky. Decent space, amicable people who actually did timely studio repairs and didn't try to shaft them. What was not to love?

They were also lucky neither the label or the clothing company knew what truly had become of Mars and how Dao was actually disfigured. Amos' quick thinking was to thank for that.

The kitchen was truly a speck of space – it was a salvaged coffee table loaded with a hot plate, a spent pan with bits of yellow rice dotted along the grease streaks, a half filled electric kettle, a sticky bottle of honey, an opened box of tea and a fair amount of used dishes. Amos checked the water level of the kettle and turned it on. Soon, it started to gurgle and hiss.

Isaiah propped his guitar against a travel case almost as tall as him and sat down on the cool, stone floor. The band's name was spray painted in silver on the rough, black sides of the case. A little dog doodle lived on the bottom corner, silver and silly, signed by "Azteca". She had bombed the case when on break from doing Amos' drums. Isaiah leaned on the case next to the doodle and checked his phone.

Between the two stacked pillars of amps, a metal door creaked open and clanged shut. Mars finally came, albeit a bit late. He used to be the first one there, fixing tea and coffee for everyone. Now, the clock didn't matter much. He was there when he was there, he wasn't when he wasn't.

The familiar, heavy footsteps snapped up Isaiah's attention. He wasn't exactly afraid but he was cautious. No one wanted to wind up like Dao.

Isaiah clambered to his feet as he greeted, warmly and loudly for Amos to hear with his baritone, gruff voice, "Mars! How ya been, man?" He was mindful not to touch his bandmate, no hugs, no daps, no accidents. It was rough welcoming Mars like a stranger, the band had been together for six years and he's known Mars longer than that. But Isaiah managed, or at least he tried to make his stilted actions look less awkward.

Amos had set out foam cups he found in a package under the table and poured out steaming hot water as he kept his ears perked. Isaiah sounded kind but nervous, Mars was quiet. Amos threw in some tea bags and announced, "Mars, I got you some tea! You, too, Isaiah. Come get some!"

Mars could see his bandmates' efforts to be warm and welcoming, but he could also hear their racing thoughts.

He's wearing a hat today, Isaiah noted, alleviated. *Thank you, God.*

Hopefully Mars is in a good mood today, Amos wondered. *Gotta get this song done and he gotta re-do his tracks.*

Mars tried to reassure them. He smiled as warmly as he could feign. "How you two doin'? Amos, what tea is it?"

Isaiah headed over to Amos as the drummer described, "It's the orange and ginger one. We low on it but got enough left for a couple days. I'll run to the store later for more."

Mars sauntered up to the packed table and picked out a cup. The warmth of the cup felt good against the chill of the air conditioning. He suggested, "Why can't Isaiah do it? He seeks out the best deals."

Isaiah paused, cup in partially tattooed hand. A light chill ran over his wiry frame.

Amos retorted, "Nah, I can do it–"

"Cuz, *Isaiah* should go." Mars insisted with a kind smile.

He wants to talk, Amos guessed. He asked the frozen guitarist, "Ey, Isaiah, you think you can do the store run? You are a coupon-master, after all. Probably come back with half the store and only spend three dollars," he lightly jabbed.

Mars chuckled along with Amos as he nibbled on his cup, "It's true, you know."

Slow to catch on, Isaiah reluctantly agreed, "Uhhhh … sure. I-I'll go now since we just took a break." He patted his black shorts to check for his keys and phone and then left. Mars wanted to talk. Alone. Isaiah just hoped the studio would still be in one piece when he got back.

Mars quietly drank his tea as the metal door creaked open and clanged shut.

Amos watched Mars for a moment. "Dude, what is going *on?*" he asked.

Mars kept drinking his tea quietly.

Irritation bit into Amos. He could tell Mars was in a mood. "Man, seriously. *Talk* to me–"

Mars pursed his lips and pulled out a curved of glass. He stared at it. Smooth, like the side of a bottle. Just like the bottle Amos lied about to the label. The memory came back to Mars, hearing his cousin say through a closed door on the phone, *Yea, it was a bottle. Nah, it wasn't on purpose, Mars' not like that .... I was* there, *that's how I know. He got passionate and threw it at the wall. Some of it hit Dao. Nah, Dao's banged up but it ain't that bad. Coulda been but thankfully, it wasn't.*

"Why can't one of these just end me already?" Mars mused, his voice flat and dead. He flickered the shard between his fingers, captivated.

Amos stepped over to pluck the shard from Mars' fingers. "Mars, stop talking like that," said Amos as he went to the trash can beside the left pillar of amps.

"Like what?" Mars asked, feigning innocence. He watched his cousin's face flash with anger as he stood beside the trash can.

"Jacob, you know what I mean!" Amos shot. He was beyond irate, Amos rarely used Mars' real name.

Mars stood there, unaffected. His face blank, he reasoned, "I'm a monster, a freak. And you know it."

Amos stalked up to Mars, "No! No, we are *not* going down this road aga–"

"I hurt Danielle this morning! What *else* does that make me?" Mars roared. His skin rumbled out a single jagged roll.

Amos threw out his hands and kept his distance. "Whoa. Whoa. Ey, Mars. Calm down, man. Just. Chill. Please be chill. *Please* chill out."

Another rumble rolled over Mars' skin as he tried to quell his nerves. His cousin's mind moved too fast to read.

Careful and cautious, Amos asked, "How ... how bad?"

Mars closed his eyes. He could see her tears and hear her watery voice. *I'm fine.*

"Mars?"

Mars willed away the feel of disgust towards himself, "Nothing … now. No blood."

Amos sighed in peace. *Thank God*, he thought. "Mars, man, you gotta work on this. You'd be better if –"

"'*Better*?" Mars spat bitterly. He approached Amos, slow and angry. They were roughly the same height but Mars' fuming made him feel even taller. Amos started to back away towards the mural. "'*Better*?" Mars caustically repeated. "You think there's a '*better*' of this that somehow don't end with my casket?"

Pressed against the mural, Amos reminded, "You gotta have faith, man! Handle this!"

Mars stopped. His face became blank again.

Amos grew concerned, "Mars, man. You okay?"

Tired, Mars asked, "Why am I like this? Why did I have to survive the explosion?"

The billion dollar question and one Mars always asked Amos at least once a month since he came home from the hospital.

It had been eight months since the accident that changed him. Mars was taking a stroll by the docks when an old chemical factory blew up beside him. There was an overlooked gas leak, thanks to the many ignored calls and requests to the city. The blast sent him over a hundred feet, covered with glass from the windows. He ended up so laden with shards, the doctors in the ICU debated whether it would be better to leave some of the glass in him as some were just too deep to get out. Mars was already in bad shape, they didn't want to risk severing additional nerves or veins to get them out. Even sedating him was hotly debated. They also toyed with the thought of taking the risk anyway and hope for the best. They decided to take out the surface shards and work as carefully as possible for the dangerous ones. They took care of removing what they could the day Mars came in but for the riskier ones, the doctors placed Mars' name on the surgery sheet for the next morning when the top surgeon could come in.

Next day, doctors found during their pre-surgery checkup that Mars was healing up fine. Whatever chemicals struck him made him heal faster than any medicine or surgery ever could. His body changed to accommodate the glass and chemicals, he even could create glass on his own. From time to time, glass would be found in his bandages or laid beside him in bed. The doctors and nurses shared the discovery with Amos and Danielle in private. They were glad that Mars was, for lack of a better word, okay but begged the hospital staff to keep this new condition secret, citing every health privacy rule and law they could think of.

Amos broke a censored version to the label, that Mars was recuperating better than the doctors guessed, thanks to having a dedicated and outstanding surgical team, a strong will and good faith. Danielle told Dao and Isaiah the truth, neither believed her until they visited Mars with Danielle and saw her pull a shard caught underneath a bandage when she tried to redress his arm as he napped. When Amos found out that they knew, he first swore and then swore them to secrecy.

The label told the fans of Lumination Rising that Mars was indeed at the fateful factory blast but his condition had stabilized and he may be moved out of the ICU soon, thanks to the amazing doctors, nurses and staff at San Diego Rivers Memorial. Since the news broke, fans piled outside daily and even more sent gifts. Sometimes, the remainder of the band would do signings outside the hospital but Mars was only greeted by hospital staff or loved ones. The day he left was quiet and in secret, ushered by his wife and cousin into a waiting car.

From that day, life radically changed.

Everyone thought it was pretty cool Mars could make glass and turn it into beautiful sculptures, especially for Danielle and their daughters. But when it was just Amos and Mars, it was a much different story. Even in the hospital, Mars would beg for Amos to kill him. "Please," he pleaded achingly when they were alone, "Put this pillow over … over my head. I don't want to live anymore. Kill me, please. You don't have to look, Amos. Just help me out." Amos never told the nurses or doctors. Amos also didn't tell them that Mars told him he tried every day to kill himself with the glass as he laid in bed but his body wouldn't allow it. Eventually, Amos just walked away when the request would come up during Mars' hospital stay. Out of the hospital, Mars would still quip to Amos from time to time, "I'm still offering."

However, Mars never ever shared to anyone that he could hear thoughts about him. They sounded like invading whispers. At first, he thought that he was hearing things but when it dawned on him what was actually happening, it made him feel even more distant and like a freak. He felt cursed and that everyone would be so much better off without him.

Isaiah drove down the sunny streets of San Diego in his beat-up car. The doors didn't match and sometimes there was an alarming cough under the hood but it still ran. Next year, he could register it as a "historic" car. Isaiah still debated on whether or not he would want to.

He headed towards a great market over in southern Chula Vista that always had the best deals, Sol Markets. Most of the product tags in the store were in Spanish but Isaiah had his parents' tongue and their knack for deals. His family was obscenely frugal but still wanted to eat and live well. None of the band members were born with silver spoons, everyone came up from hard-working families, but Isaiah had a special skill to stretch a dollar when it came to food and supplies.

Dao was on the phone, his deep voice loud and clear through the old speakers. They crackled from time to time. Isaiah's aux cord was on its last leg, covered in a thick cast of electrical tape at the plugs, but still worked well enough. He had been on the phone with Dao since he first called him as soon as he got in the car.

"Bro, don't forget to get the snack cookies I like," Dao commented, interrupting himself on a previous subject he was talking about.

Taking a left turn, Isaiah asked, "The red ones with the cherry in them?"

"I thought they were raspberries?"

Isaiah shrugged. The sun beamed on his skin, covered with musical art. His silver curls gleamed in the sunlight. "I 'on't know. Maybe they got both."

"Oooh, get Viper!" Dao threw in, "The black can."

Isaiah snickered, "I ain't gettin' that for you, man. That stuff is straight basura, holmes. Energy drinks get you too live, man."

"Energy drinks *keep* me alive, man. Especially Viper. Nectar of the gods," Dao rebuffed playfully.

"Sayeth the Black Buddhist. I thought you supposed to reject material stuff and stuff," Isaiah reminded as he waited for the light to change.

"Hey," Dao remarked with mock defensiveness, "I'm still a work in progress. And get the gold can instead."

The light changed, and Isaiah was back on the move as he suggested, "How about you get one of those smoothie drinks? Healthier for you."

Dao thought on it for a second. Then he said, "Viper got a version called Viper: The Garden. Two birds, one stone."

"And no hits, you are *not* gonna be bouncing off the walls when you come back. You just gonna be a half blind Speedy Gonzalez. No way." Isaiah laughed, Dao didn't.

"How long do we have to turn in the album?" Dao asked.

Isaiah noticed the change in subject and mentally kicked himself for the faux pas, "Savalez is giving us to the fall, it looks like. We got an extension so you can get better but he wants us out there and touring. He wants us to get on Dowry's level."

Dao moaned, "Maaaaaaan, The Dowry Effect just a *machine*. All them chicks, straight up moving day and night. Complete Terminators, all of them. Do *any* of those girls ever sleep?"

Isaiah shrugged as he waited for a pedestrian to cross the street. He was in no rush. He was certain if Mars leveled the studio, showing up in the aftermath was far safer than arriving during the action. "I honestly have *no* idea but they crank out records and tours at a rate Savalez *loves*."

Dao joked, "I guess Punk isn't really dead."

Isaiah broke into a fit of hearty laughter, "Better not be or we are partially *screwed*. If not *completely*. You know I'm deathly allergic to Pop."

The bassist laughed, "I think we all are."

The dingy red roof of the store broke over the horizon as Isaiah reminisced, "Remember when we got our first Grammy ballots? I just wrote random swear words on mine. Ain't you draw the middle finger on yours or was that Amos?"

"Me but Amos drew a butt on his," Dao confirmed.

"Mars sent his in half torched …" Isaiah trailed off. He had waded back into acidic waters once again. Isaiah turned into the sparse parking lot. Plenty of customers but few cars.

A bus on the curb briefly stopped, dropping off a few more shoppers.

Dao blustered a long, loud sigh. "How am I going to do this?" He muttered to himself.

"How you gonna do what?" Isaiah asked as he found a spot close to the front door.

Dao stammered, caught off guard, "I – ehhhhh – I dunno–"

"Spit it out, man," Isaiah turned the car off, it sputtered quiet. He snatched out the aux cord and brought the phone to his ear. The case was covered with bumpy, colorful sugar skulls.

"I was …. I might come in tomorrow?"

Isaiah was floored with joy. "Dude, that's amazing! Did your doctor say you could?" Isaiah got out the car, the roaring heat that met him made him glad his A/C didn't conk again. Last summer was torture and the repairs equaled an extra long tour he was already sick of half way through. The guitarist wasted no time getting under the shade of the canopy of a melon stall outside the store and went inside.

"Nah," Dao answered. "Just bored. I just can't do nothin' there, though."

Inside Sol Markets, Isaiah murmured close to the phone, "What about M, though?"

Dao gave it a moment's ponder. He sighed again, "I 'on't know, bro. I … I just can't face him yet. Has he gotten better about his … condition?"

Isaiah tugged at a curl or two in thought. He weighed between telling a sweet lie or the bitter truth as he grabbed a red, worn shopping basket and started towards the produce section that lined the long wall. He came clean, "I 'on't know, man. Nothing much else happened since but A knows better than me." Isaiah always shortened the names of his band members since the one day he got mobbed by a small horde of fans at a flower shop about a year ago. As if his silver hair, countless tattoos and gruff voice couldn't make him stand out enough, someone overheard him on the phone as he flipped through a sales book. "I think you'll be fine if A is around. I'll make sure you stick to him like glue. M wears hats more, too. We've found far less … 'stuff' since that."

"Hmmm," Dao considered. It had already been almost a month since his injury. And this album needs to be finished – the sooner, the better. Downloads and streams don't keep musicians fed, tours do. "I'll try. At least get in around two. I'll catch you later, ok?"

"See ya, man. Feel better, ok?" Isaiah picked up a pineapple and weighed it in his hand. Fairly round and pretty heavy, Isaiah calculated the price in his head and tried to find a lighter one just as thick.

"Sure thing", Dao hung up. His phone sat in a charging port that mimicked a red rotary phone but had the smartphone in the place of the dial. He wanted to come back, being home dulled him to tears. But facing Mars again… Dao headed up the stairs of his small home. A little house on a quiet street, what he always wanted.

Minutes later, the phone bleated an impressive funk tune with jarring trumpets. The screen read "Savalez the Overlord".

Dao hurried back into the living room. The phone rang loud atop his old, tall amp. He was in the middle of changing the bedding in his hamster's cage. Dao thundered down the stairs, lined with family pictures and gold records. He kept a careful hand over his pet, Chunks, as the little gray hamster rode his shoulder. He snatched up the receiver on the last ring.

"Hola, Savalez." It was almost a third of the entire extent of Dao's Spanish, outside of the swears and insults the rest of the band taught him.

Savalez replied with a warm drawl, "Dao! How are you? How is your eye?"

The warmth unsettled Dao a bit. Savalez rarely made cordial calls just to chit-chat. And whenever Savalez called with a voice so warm, something was hot on his mind.

"Everything is good so far. Doc said I'm getting better–"

"Oh! So you'll be 20/20 in both eyes again? And the scars are soon gonna disappear?" Savalez questioned.

Dao winced at the back-handed compliment. "The eye is gonna stay busted and so will my face." He petted Chunks out of self-comfort, who happily chewed away on a near dreadlock. Dao attempted to stream the dread from Chunks' nibbling paws as he asked, "Is everything fine?"

"Absolutely *lovely*," Savalez reassured. "I just wanted to check in on you as you healed. You know how everyone is familia to me. When Mars was in the hospital, I did the same."

Dao nodded, "Ah, okay. I'm doin' good. Writing up some tabs and always in the kitchen with something new. I can't sit around doing nothing," he laughed. Dao hoped it would be enough to placate Savalez.

The label head laughed with Dao, "That's good, that's good, Dao! Always good to hear that. Don't work yourself too hard, getting better is priority."

"I agree." Dao wondered where the conversation would turn next.

"Dao," Savalez inquired, "how *are* things in Lumination? You and Mars good? Amos said it was an accident with the bottle – was it a bottle or a glass? I forget."

"Bottle," Dao piped. How could he forget? Amos drilled him over and over again even in the hospital until he knew the tale by heart: Glass bottle. Mars threw it out of passion while singing – *no* malevolence intended whatsoever. Dao accidently got caught in the spray of shards. Mars is entirely innocent and regretful. And does not have any unusual abilities of any kind. Perfectly normal. And happy. And *normal*.

"Ahhhh, yes, I think Amos *did* say 'bottle'," Savalez said. "Forgive me, I'm old."

"It's fine. All is good between Mars and I. He wouldn't stop apologizing," Dao lied. Mars had hardly said anything that could even barely resemble an apology, even a scarce one. Either too busy brooding or Amos would pipe up and speak for Mars instead. If anything, it was Amos who apologized over and over. Or attempted to suppress the topic altogether.

"Wonderful," Savalez replied, pleased. "You two are like brothers, I don't want any bad blood happening. Especially as this album is coming out. If all goes well, this could go far. I wanna make sure everyone is happy during the whole trip."

"I get it, I get it," said Dao, stuffing his true feelings. He took Chunks from his shoulder and stroked the hamster's soft coat with his long thumb. Chunks nuzzled his palm. "I'm healing fine – not perfectly but fine – and everything between Mars and I is fine."

"'Fine'," Savalez snorted. He resumed his lovely tone, "As long as everything is 'fine'. I'll let you get back to your day, okay?"

"Okay," said Dao. "Bye bye."

"Talk to you later." Savalez hung up.

Dao returned the receiver and rubbed his head. He ruffled his thin dreads, "Chunks, you are *so* lucky you do not have to put up with people-problems." He petted Chunks with his other hand as he started back up the stairs. "The worst you have to think about is how many spare treats you can sucker out of my brother, Slice. Whatever Savalez called for, it better not bite us later. Hmph, knowin' Amos, I'm probably gonna have *new* lines to learn. More lines, more lies."

Isaiah returned to the studio, clusters of shopping bags in tow. He figured it was best to replenish everything that needed replenishing. And it was quite a bit.

He found Amos and Mars sitting around the drum-set. Mars' tahm was off, his dreads freely cascaded down his back. Isaiah was taken aback as Amos jumped up and tried to explain.

"He got hot! He was getting hot!" Amos rattled off as he stepped over stools, instruments and junk to reach a rattled Isaiah, who was riveted to the spot. "It's fine! He's been sitting in the same place and whatever shards fell out, I got up!" Amos pulled the shopping bags from Isaiah's loose hands. "It's fine, I swear!" Amos called over to his cousin behind him, "Mars, cover it up!"

Mars simply watched, unmoved.

"He – he ain't doin' it," Isaiah reported, hazel eyes glued on Mars' blank expression.

Amos turned around, bags in hand. He fussed, "We *talked* about this, Mars! *Just* talked about this. Put them *up*, that was the agreement! Isaiah is here now!"

Without care, Mars picked up his tahm from his lap and slid it on. He made sure to get every tendril. A shard of glass fell from the mess of hair and tinkered audibly onto the floor.

Amos tried to hurry towards the shard but Mars quietly and languidly picked it up. He looked at the new jagged piece, straight and sharp. Before he could close his hand around it, Amos clutched it from his palm and threw it away, bags rustling along on his thick, sailor tatted wrists.

Mars looked on and held his hands up. "Isaiah, I'm harmless now," the vocalist blandly joked.

Amos sat the bags down around the kitchen area. He marveled at the swollen bounty of goods and wanted to change the subject. "Isaiah! How much was all of this?" Isaiah was quiet, still frozen by the door. Amos beckoned him over, "Isaiah! Mars is safe, man! Come over!"

Timid and meek, Isaiah paced closer and closer to Amos, as if Mars was a hungry tiger Amos swore he fed. Isaiah still could see the holes in the nearby amps and remembered how Dao was in front of him as Mars threw his head about in passion during the practice of a thrash metal song. With his dreads flying about, no one could predict what had happened next, how Dao snapped his head away and started clutching his face. Isaiah saw Dao stumble towards him, his faded red bass thumped against his pained gait. Before Isaiah could even understand what had happened, Dao crumpled to the floor, screaming and freely bleeding through his hands and his spindly, black dreads. Not a day passed where the haunting realization didn't cross Isaiah's mind that if Dao wasn't there, that would have been him.

Beside Amos like a duckling to a goose, Isaiah never took his eyes off Mars. *Why'd Amos let Mars take his hat off? Dao's gonna be here tomorrow.*

Mars smiled at Isaiah, chilling the guitarist further.

Amos repeated himself, "Isaiah, how much was all of this?"

"Uh … ehhh … it was …," Isaiah rustled through the bags, looking for the receipt. In the least packed bag of raspberry fritters, Isaiah found the long strip, peach bars ran down half the length. He could feel Mars' unsettling stare, "Thirteen seventy-five."

"Thirteen seventy-five!" Amos marveled. "For all this?"

"Told you Isaiah was a good idea," Mars quipped, beaming.

Amos patted Isaiah warmly on the back. "Good job, dude! I'mma go put some of these away." The drummer picked up a tall block of toilet paper and a stack of paper plates. To get a better handle on the toilet paper, Amos sat down the paper plates and headed to the bathroom on the other side of the small studio, an emerald painted wooden door almost right next to the blue metal double doors that led to the storage warehouse.

Now, Isaiah was alone with Mars. This used to be fine, Mars had the sunniest of personalities. But since the explosion, a more … enraptured person replaced him.

"How's Dao?" Mars asked with a pop of interest.

"'Dao'?" echoed Isaiah, his blood turned cold.

"Yes, 'Dao'. Our bassist? How is he doing?" Mars wore a polite smile.

Isaiah stammered, "He's … h-he doin' good. Misses playin-playin wi-with us."

"Hmm," Mars said pensively. "When will he be back?"

Isaiah fettered out an anxious, breathy laugh as he rubbed his hands and tugged his curls. Mars idly watched. Amos returned with the empty plastic bag crumpled up in his hand.

"Hey, Amos! Just in time! Dao told me he plans to swing by tomorrow," Isaiah announced far louder than he needed to. Mars smirked but Amos stood stunned.

Dude, Mars *is here!* Amos panicked internally. "Dude, that's cool!" he cheered with a bright smile. Amos asked Mars, "How do you feel about this?"

"How am I *allowed* to feel?" the vocalist shrugged. Mars could tell he was getting a little better at reading thoughts. They were still no louder than whispers but they were clearer. Mars promised, "I'll try to be on my best behavior. Put me down if I get too much."

A sinking feeling pulled at Amos. He tired of his cousin's melancholy but it kept coming back. "Mars, ain't no one gonna put you down. You're fine, man. You ain't a monster, Mars."

The vocalist got up. "Sure, Amos. I'm gonna go lay down my tracks. I'll be in the Sound Box … hat off." Mars walked to the small, black room nestled in the corner of the studio space, a dark, felt covered cube jutting out from the wall that shared the same wall as the doors to the warehouse. Self-contained, it had its own computer and padding for ease of a single person to record and produce themselves. It had a few pockmarks in the egg foam lining but nothing worse than that.

Amos wanted to suggest the hat should stay on for cleaner recording in case shards came out but thought to the better of it. *Mars would take it the wrong way,* Amos believed. Instead, he waited for Mars to close the padded door of the

Sound Box and the blue "Recording" light to pop on over the door.

Without a moment's pause, Amos whisked about to interrogate Isaiah, "What the *holy* hell were you thinking?! Mars was here and you freakin' announced Dao showin' up like it's *nothin*? We *plan* first, *then* tell Mars! Why'd you do this, man?"

"He put me on the spot, man!" Isaiah defended.

Amos was exasperated. He rubbed his face and stared up at the plywood and egg foam ceiling. He preferred to stay a step ahead of Mars when he could but now it was time to improvise.

"Amos, I'm *sorry*," Isaiah pleaded. He knew the protocol, he just couldn't do it this time. "I told Dao he's gonna stay close by you, no matter what. Make sure that happens, okay?"

Harried, Amos rustled his close-cut onyx hair. He had no other choice but to go with the makeshift plan. "Okay," he haplessly agreed and licked his lips in thought. Amos didn't think this was the best of plans but it was miles better than having none at all.

Night came quickly. Mars was home, seated at an oblong table filled with warmth and cheer as he and his family had dinner. He was all smiles and still had on his street clothes, including his tahm. Mars had prepared soup for his family but before the girls were called, Danielle checked every bowl for a random shard with a strainer. Mars had to stand by in marked resignation.

At the dinner table, Mars asked his daughters about their day as Danielle ate.

"So!" He perked with a light clap, "What did you both learn? Vivica? Violet?"

The younger of the two, Violet, piped up first. "We learned shapes! I can draw a rumpus now!"

Danielle and Mars snickered to themselves.

Mars warmly corrected, "I think you mean 'rhombus', Violet. Are you gonna show Daddy later after dinner?"

The child nodded, her little barrettes on the end of her black braids clinked against the ceramic soup bowl and bounced off her tawny brown cheeks. She had the bright, kind eyes of her father and the wider nose of her mother, just like her sister. Amos still swore to this very day that they both had his firm eyebrows. Vivica was a grade older than her sister and with a plumper face. She had lost a tooth last month. Her father created a glittering glass capsule to put the tooth in. When she woke up, there was a twenty-dollar bill in its stead. She wanted to buy ice cream with it. Violet had a vivacious spirit, she always loved being first. She also loved the small tiaras she would beg her dad to put on her head. Especially if she got good grades, which was often.

Vivica, not to be outdone by her little sister, announced, "We're learning subtraction with three numbers now!"

Charmed and intrigued, Danielle asked, "Really? What is three hundred subtracted from two hundred and fifteen?"

Vivica thought for a while. Violet wanted to answer for

her but Danielle quieted her before she could blurt the answer. A bit unsure, Vivica answered, "...Eighty-five?"

"Good girl!" Mars praised.

Vivica proudly beamed at her parents in satisfaction. Violet grew restless in her seat.

"Daddy," Violet chimed, "can you make a birdy? Like the one on your shoulder?"

Danielle cleared her throat. Memories of the morning swept back to her. She tried to resume the morning like normal: gather the kids, drop them off at school, pretend nothing is wrong. Only once she was back at the empty house did she mourn what had happened.

Mars said to his daughter, "Only if it's okay with Mommy." He asked his wife, "How about it, Dani? It'll be a small bird."

Danielle nodded as she took a sip of water. She stopped having ice in her cup since Mars came home. Just to be safe, she always told herself.

Vivica chimed in immediately, "Daddy, can you make a doggy? I like the long ones!"

Both girls tried to pronounce the dog breed.

"Dash ... dashihound," Violet tried.

"Das'hound," Vivica attempted.

Mars was tickled by them both. He loved his girls more than anything in the world, all three of them. As Danielle tried to help them pronounce the breed correctly, Mars cupped his hands on the table into a dome. It took some concentration but soon, he could feel a formation coming true beneath his hands. And then another, taking up the remaining space. He revealed them slowly, two crystal glass figurines of a dachshund and a sparrow. The dachshund had a tilted head and a lolling tongue hanging out. The sparrow was small and delicate, with detailed, folded wings, just like the red one on the back of his shoulder.

The girls exploded into excitement. Mars passed the sparrow to Violet, who adored her father's gift. She turned the sparrow in her hands over and over, admiring every detail.

Before Mars handed the dog over, he asked once more, "What kind of dog is this?"

"Dash-hound!" Vivica bubbled, bobbing in her chair. Her aluminum foil ended braids clattered about in her ponytail.

"Dash-house!" Violet answered.

Danielle chuckled as Mars passed the dog figurine to his overjoyed daughter. Enraptured by the detail, Vivica twirled the dachshund in her hands, taking in every curve, every outline.

Nights like these were always welcomed in the small house of Juarez. A little bit of normalcy. Mars and Danielle worked hard to hide his depression and melancholic behavior. He didn't want his daughters to see him as a monster but as "special". That's how Danielle described him to them before he came home: "Daddy's a little special now. But he's still the same."

Mars and Danielle wished this serenity stretched to the rest of their lives but Mars simply couldn't bring himself to it. He was just putting on airs to save face. To make this normal would be to accept his abilities as normal. And Mars would never accept that. He couldn't.

The rest of the night was filled with love and jubilation. They had already finished their homework with Danielle, who stayed at home to care for them. Mars made tiaras and crystal draperies to turn the living room into an ice castle, the home teemed with mirth and warmth. Nights like these filled Danielle with hope for her family, especially for her husband.

As bedtime drew closer, the crystal draperies receded. The girls complained but off to bed they went. The dachshund and sparrow joined the rest of their growing menagerie in their room. Then Danielle and Mars retired to bed themselves. Mars sank deep into his pillow, eaten by a crashing wave of sorrow. Danielle laid rigid next to her husband and hoped for a better tomorrow.

The next day, Dao arrived at the studio, two PM sharp. He used to enter with a blow of energy and his usual proud declaration, "I'm *here!*" Instead, he just texted Amos and waited outside the metal door. Pads of gauze still lined the side of his thick neck, hidden by the upturned collar of his black jacket. It was a mismatch for the hot, humid weather but Dao didn't want anyone to see his scars. His dreads covered half his face, obscuring his covered eye. To avoid contact between his hair and wounds, Dao hunched himself over a bit. He appeared like a huddled giant trying to brace the cold instead of a sweltering man trying not to faint in the heat. At least his car had impeccable air conditioning.

Amos came to the door and looked outside. Finding Dao huddled but smiling, Amos' face brightened.

"You came!" Amos delighted. Seeing Dao's jacket, Amos ushered him in quickly, "Sheesh, come inside! We have A/C! You must be burning up!"

Dao grinned as he came inside, it felt wonderful to be appreciated and missed. Minutes passed like hours at home, he couldn't wait to be back. Dao thought he would have gone bonkers sitting alone in his house eating snacks, feeding his hamster and watching TV. If he wouldn't have gone mad from the boredom, his brother Slice would have given him the proper push. Dao loved his big brother but Slice made for a frustrating caretaker. Overfeeds Chunks, tries to slip meat into his meals, chats his ears off about the thrilling wonders of being a middle school teacher. Dao could hardly take it. As for online, he stayed off social media for the most part and he had asked the label to stay quiet about his injury. He'd rather unveil himself at a show. Besides, Amos told him the version he fed to the label and Dao didn't want to harm the story in any way. Lumination Rising already had enough headaches, no need to add the truth.

Though Dao was ecstatic to be back, Mars was on his mind. Back when the bassist was getting treated at Huerta Trinity Hospital, Amos visited to tell him it wasn't Mars' fault. *He's learning his new self still,* was what the drummer told him. *Nothing intentional, you know Mars ain't like that.* To be honest, Dao saw everything as Amos just trying to protect his cousin, his blood, at all costs. Dao always trusted Amos but he never forgot that.

Isaiah spotted Dao walking through the door behind Amos. He was hard to miss: tall, broad shouldered, and smiling face half covered with gauze. Mars was in the Sound Box doing his vocals. *Thank God*, thought Isaiah. This gave him enough calm to welcome Dao heartily.

He rose up from the amp he sat on in the kitchen area, arms outstretched. There was a half-eaten box of pizza Amos heated earlier propped open on the table. Isaiah walked to Dao and hugged him on his left shoulder, careful not to disturb the bandages on the right.

"Dao, man!" Isaiah elated. "You're here! You're really here!"

Dao cracked a warm smile, mostly from the left side of his mouth. The right started to hurt, as it did from time to time, especially when pulled by expression.

Isaiah's smile faltered a little at the lopsided grin. "You doin' all right?"

Amos stood beside the two, attentive and vigilant. He didn't know how Dao would be since he was back. The amps still had holes from that day, Mars wasn't much better and Isaiah had been jumpy all day, probably ruminating on the worst.

Dao clapped Isaiah's small shoulder, "I'm good. I just gotta take it easy. That's all. Just wanna get out the house for a bit and I haven't seen y'all in a while." He scanned the studio for a place to sit but also for Mars. Clear of the vocalist, Dao spotted the faded peach couch that sat in the center of the studio. It was an old, well-used lounge couch from one of Mindware's stores half a town over. Dao made his way over to sit. The other two followed suit.

Striding over, Dao proclaimed, "I'mma just do here what I do at home: sit on my butt and watch." He plopped down and sheared off his jacket to embrace the chill. Goosebumps covered his hefty muscles and sheets of tattoos. Comfortable, Dao asked, "What'd I miss?"

Isaiah plopped down beside him, "Nothing."

Amos stood before them, keeping an eye on The Sound Box. The recording light was still on. "Mars is still a bit off but better about precautions now," he informed.

Isaiah rolled his eyes. "More tahms now but Amos here sometimes lets him air out his scalp."

The drummer shot a steely look at Isaiah. Isaiah returned an annoyed look.

"Wait … *what?*" Dao was astonished. Maybe coming in wasn't the greatest plan. Maybe he should have waited … after Mars would be tied up in the snuggest strait jacket, locked away perhaps in the tightest psych ward. Preferably somewhere very, *very* far away. Dao was close to Mars, knew him for years, well before Lumination. Loved him dearly. But the man was unhinged.

Amos asserted, "Isaiah, I was *watching* him. Dao, don't stress yourself, he's got a tahm on now. I only let Mars take his hat off yesterday because he got too hot–"

"What if he uses the same excuse today?" Isaiah rebutted defiantly.

"Isaiah, *please*." Amos demanded. "Bro, don't give me that. Please don't. Mars is having a hard time. I keep pressin' on him, he's gonna have bits of glass comin' out everywhere–"

"'Everywhere'?" Mars repeated. He was out of the Sound Box. He had on a red and brown tahm and a mocking smile. Dao slid down in his seat. Mars greeted with a light air of phony politeness, "Hey, Dao. When you come in?"

Isaiah slid down alongside Dao. Amos stood rigid, face blank with a caught stare.

With a derisive smirk, Mars waved on obligingly, "No, please continue, Amos. Go on. I'm a shrapnel bomb, might as well warn them."

"Mars ..." Amos began weakly. "Please don't start. Please."

"Alvin 'Amos' Zavala," Mars seethed. He spat, "You always gotta play Safety-Safety, huh?"

Dao and Isaiah pulled their legs up, tucked themselves onto the couch and waited for the worst.

"Dude, you are *not* a monster," Amos threw back. "Stop trying to turn yourself into one–"

Mars shot a spike of glass into the ground. It pierced the cement floor with a sickening, clear crunch. Isaiah and Dao jumped at the sound. Amos was weary.

The drummer sighed, "Still don't make you a monster. You don't kill–"

"Yet–"

"At *all*. Mars, I've known you as long as I've been alive. This ain't you, man," Amos said, exasperated. Mars still stared at him with cold, steady eyes. Amos looked at Dao and Isaiah curled up flat on the couch. Both of them had the same terrified expression.

Isaiah mouthed to Amos, "What are you *doing?*" *Mars is out of his mind!* He fretted. *Amos tryna get us all killed?*

"I wonder the same, Isaiah," Mars said. He chortled a bit. "I can read thoughts a little bit. But only a *little.* Especially if it's about *me.*"

The guitarist's eyes grew wide at Amos. Dao kept himself tucked as well as he could. It ebbed him some pain but he tried not to care. Better than being struck again.

Amos simply didn't understand. "What?"

"You heard me, cuz," Mars announced, as if he wanted the whole world to hear. "I've been listening on and off since I've left the hospital! I never meant to hurt Dao – It was an honest mistake, Dao!" Mars called out to the frightened bassist.

He's gonna kill me, ain't he? Dao feared. He clutched onto Isaiah's hand.

"But you still don't believe me," Mars continued. "Do you?" Mars shot another shard into the ground, this one more jagged and longer than the first.

Isaiah sprang up, arms thrown out. "Mars! *Stop!*" He was part irritated, part terrified. "What do you *want,* dude? Do you wanna be scary? Fine, you're scary right now! Is that it?"

Amos seconded, "Mars, ain't *nothin'* 'bout your powers – or whatever they are – scary by themselves. Hell, you could help me finally fix that stupid window in my house. But you're all off safety, man."

Mars was unfazed. His skin started to become jagged.

Isaiah dropped back down onto the couch. He curled up and covered his head. Dao tucked in more, some of the gauze pads strained against the back of his neck. He hoped none of his wounds would reopen.

Muffled by his knees, Isaiah yelled out, "Why can't we have old Mars back? Why you gotta be so dark now?"

Amos shrugged, listless, "Isaiah's right. If you wanna go ham, just do it now. Savalez already calls us 'Spinal Tap' as a joke when we ain't around. At least we won't have to worry about that album anymore." *I guess he wants to be the monster that bad, huh?* pondered Amos. He couldn't help but feel hopeless. He wanted the old Mars back, too.

Mars' skin softened. Confused, he asked, "Why aren't you scared?"

"Mars, I know you far too well," Amos tossed out. "You gotta read my mind but I don't have to read yours. This whole experience got you messed up and we're all here tryna cope. I ain't scared – I'm tired! Bro, you know how many stories I had to spin to the label about *ev-ry-thing* goin' on with you? They don't know about the glass, they don't know the truth about Dao's *injury*, none of it!" Amos rubbed his head, "You tryna play monster, I'm playin' spin doctor. Does it mean so much for people to be scared of you? Seriously? Look around! Isaiah and Dao are huddled up on this here couch, you shootin' glass javelins into the floor, is this really Lumination Rising?"

Amos held out a hand over the couch. He invited, "C'mon, cuz. Don't be like that. You're not a monster. You just gotta learn how to control your abilities better."

Isaiah lifted his head a little, just enough to peek over the back of the couch. Dao remained hidden.

The guitarist emptied his heart, "Mars. I wouldn't get so freaked if you controlled your stuff more, man." He tried to joke, "We'd save so much money on merch if you could make it."

Silence. The joke fell flat. Isaiah sank back down.

He shrugged, huddled up, "I tried."

Dao praised quietly, "You did good, man."

Amos still had his arm out. "Are you with us? Or against us? You're choosing, *now*."

Mars stood there, unsure. No way did he want to be a monster but his changes made him feel like one. Hearing the thoughts of the people he loved about him convinced him that he was one. The fear everyone had of him was drowning.

"I … I can't be the old Mars," he forfeited.

Amos rolled his eyes, hand still out. He went around the couch and walked over to Mars to grab his wrist. "We know. That Mars didn't have glass coming out of him, but he was nicer. We can get *that* out of you." Amos pulled Mars to the couch as he continued, "You're still the same person, just a different body."

1.2

Six months had passed. The album was nearly done, titled *Throwing Stones*. The holes in the floor were covered up with a rug and a couple stacked amps. Dao's bandages were off, deep scars marred the right side of his face and neck, his eye was clouded. He could smile and pivot his head freely but he still kept his dreads over half his face. He tried to resume normalcy but he still found being around Mars difficult. No matter what Amos did to keep the peace, Dao struggled to get past the slight that disfigured him.

Mars had been away for four months at Amos's house. He told his wife and children that he would be gone for a little bit. The daughters sobbed and cried, but Danielle understood. She wasn't happy but she understood. Mars' melancholy became harder to keep under wraps at home. There were days she feared coming home to a corpse. Amos promised her that he would do all that he could to get Mars back on his feet and in control of his abilities. Everyone was grateful for their pint-sized fame or even this would not have been possible. No one wanted Mars' condition somehow leaked out to the world.

The first weeks were the hardest. Mars drowned in his depression. He wanted to go home. He wanted to be left alone. He wanted death. He wanted to be normal again. Amos worked night and day to bring Mars around, to prove that he was not a monster. Danielle visited every Tuesday and Wednesday, after dropping the kids off at school. She wanted to see him more but Amos restricted it, he wanted Mars to get a bit better – at least to safely hug without any risk of shards. That took three months.

During the stay, there was one particularly trying night. It was two months in, Mars and Amos were home alone, eating dinner. The day was done, another successful day at the studio. Tracks were laid, no one died, minimal glass found (one found in Amos' cup among the ice), roaring success. They ate at the small kitchen table, a rule Amos instituted so he could ensure Mars wouldn't try to swallow a fallen shard – he had learned the hard way in the beginning when they would eat together on the couch in front of the television and Mars fell over with a small stream of blood dribbled from the corner of his mouth. Amos knew Mars couldn't be harmed by his own glass but that that didn't stop his cousin from trying. Several times, Amos caught Mars trying to force his body to reject the glass and let it slice him. It left a bloody mess each and every time.

Amos' home was simple and small. The walls were lined with all of Lumination Rising's achievements, positive articles about him and family pictures. His decor was quaint but lively, he loved colors. Many things in his house were mismatched, except for his wooden dining room set. Amos simply liked to live comfortably. Mars living there sometimes impinged on the comfort that was Amos' home. For one, Amos no longer could just plop down on the couch after a long day of practice anymore. Shard checks were constant and plenty.

The dining room was beautiful but too crowded with wooden cabinets filled with fine ceramic plates, some adorned with moving Spanish scriptures, some detailed with vivacious colored skulls or old Chinese calligraphy paintings. Framed drawings and portraits of great Chicanos and Afro-Latin people in history were dotted between the plates. The long table was ornate but difficult for Amos to keep a proper eye on Mars, so they ate at the small kitchen round table instead.

The kitchen was just as nice as the dining room but not as stuffed with trinkets and things. A single orb hung by a single black chain illuminated the kitchen. It was handmade, a large, drizzled web of crystal sea blue resin. Italian wedding soup simmered on the blotchy stove, something Isaiah made and brought over earlier in the week. It was less of an act of kindness and more of an act of sloughing off extra soup. He had made too much.

Amos sat almost opposite of Mars at the round table. The drummer was almost done with his soup and gnawed on a piece of thick sliced bread. Mars simply gazed at his plate, sullen and lifeless. He had only eaten half of his soup and never touched his bread. His fingers dawdled in his lap under the table, they played with a hidden shard that slipped out of his palm.

Amos looked up at Mars, he noticed that his cousin had been quiet all evening. Even at practice, he was a bit more muted than normal. "Mars, dude," he said, "you wanna talk about how today was?"

Mars hissed out a tired sigh and shifted his jaw in thought. He hated this part, the fact he had to talk about his day everyday so Amos could pick it apart. Amos called it "improving control", Mars considered it invasive, stupid, and annoying.

Amos took another bite of bread as he leaned back and beckoned, "C'mon, holmes. You know you gotta do this. You been quiet *all* day. What's goin' on right now?"

Mars flickered the small shard between his fingers. He replied, his voice dull, "Nothin', man. Normal day, still breathin'." He shot an irritated smile, "Happy?"

Amos rolled his eyes. "Man, please don't be like that. I'm just tryna help yo–"

"You *aren't* tryna help me," Mars accused, "you're *trying* to keep me alive."

Mars got up and walked away.

Amos spotted the small shard between Mars' fingers as he sauntered into the living room, where the television played a random silly sitcom, bathing the couch with dancing light. He darted out of his chair and dashed in front of his cousin. Amos stuck out a waiting hand and demanded, "I saw that, give it to me. You got a shard in your left hand."

Mars' face was bored and unchanged. He thought of

swallowing it for a moment but instead he said, "Why? It's who I am." He held up the shard. Its jagged edges glinted against the brilliant white that filled the room. "Just drag this across my throat–"

"Stop *talkin'* like that!" Amos grabbed at the shard but Mars clutched his wrist and spun him around until Amos' back struck the wall of the archway that connected the kitchen and dining room. Amos almost unhinged the long calendar he was reared into. Fire burned in his eyes as he spat at Mars, "You know I'm not gonna do that, you're my cousin and I care–"

"What about Dao!" Mars roared. One of his dreads rose, its end sharpened to a point with a dart of glass, and shot into the wall beside Amos' ear. Amos flinched when the dread lodged into the wall, bits of drywall tumbled down.

Mars heard Amos swear at the near miss in his mind. It made him smile wickedly. "What's the matter, cuz? Am I still *normal*? Am I still *safe* to be around?"

Amos tilted himself to leave but another sharpened dread lunged into the wall on his other side, just an inch off from his temple. He could hear the pop of plaster breaking as it struck. "Mars! Stop!" he demanded. "Stop this *now!*"

"Why?" Mars face still bore a terrible grin, "I'm just being my new self–"

"You're just tryna paint yourself as the bad guy!" Amos refused. "This ain't you! This ain–"

Three more dreads lodged themselves into the wall around Amos' shoulders and neck. One was quite close, Amos could feel the glass-hardened hair of the dread brush against the side of his neck. There was a subtle slice of pain that bled up soon after.

"I could have *killed* Dao, you know that, right?" Mars said, both his tone and expression flat. "And here you are, taking care of me. Strugglin' to keep me alive. For what? So I can do it again?"

Amos spoke over the end of Mars words, "You're not *like* that! It was a *mistake*–"

"How do you know?" Mars seethed. "I'm the one that can read minds, not you. How do you know?"

Another dread lodged into the wall. It was a bit further away than the rest but still threateningly close to Amos' elbow. Amos flinched slightly.

Mars presented the small shard in his hand to Amos' eyes. "This little thing. This–"

"I knew you all your life, Mars," Amos answered with a subtle quake in his voice. *Mars is going overboard, I gotta calm him down*, he thought.

"Just end me, it's pretty simple," Mars summed. "Dao will be safe. Isaiah will have nothing to fear. Savalez will be a bit pissed but I'm sure you'll dredge up some half-cocked story that saves us all."

"What about Dani and the kids?" Amos asked. "You think they won't miss you?"

Mars' eyes glassed over with tears. "They'll be better off without me, you know that."

Amos shook his head, "No, no they won't, you know tha–"

"They *will!*" Mars roared. Amos turned his head from

the fury. "They *have* to," Mars whispered as a tear rolled down his cheek. He quaked, "Dani's *scared* of me, I can hear it in her *mind*. She's *afraid* of me. I can't *do* that to her, you know I can't." He dropped his head and sniffed, "I love her too much to stick around. She doesn't deserve what I am right now. She needs to have better. Her *and* the girls." Mars looked up, his cheeks rouge and wet, "They all deserve so much better than me right now."

Amos threaded through the lanced dreads to slip his arms around his cousin's neck and hug him. He could feel Mars' skin begin to churn defensively at the touch. Amos patted his back, "I know you don't wanna hurt Dani or the girls. That's why you're here with me. So we can get you back. I can't read Dani's mind but I know she misses you like crazy. She tells me all the time. The girls miss you, too."

Mars bawled into a wailing cry. It was rare for Amos to see Mars so broken down but he wasn't surprised. He let Mars have his shoulder, to sob and be frustrated.

Amos walked Mars away from the wall. His lanced dreads slipped out, each of them covered with albus dust and bits of plaster. They tinkered together as they slapped to Mars' side.

Mars rattled, "Just kill me already, Amos. I promise I'll make it easy for you. I won't struggle. I won't do anything. I'll just …. Please just do it. Stop pretending you're not scared of me and just *do* it already."

Amos sighed. "Mars, you know I won't do that. I can't just kill my own cousin. How could I *live* with that–"

"That you did me a favor–"

"That I murdered someone I *love*," Amos persisted. "I've been mad at you before. Tons and tons of times. But never *ever* would I ever want to kill you. Knock some sense into you, sure. Murder you? *Never.* It just isn't happening. I couldn't live with *myself* if so, Mars. And you know that. You *know* that would eat me up alive."

Mars sniffed, "But why? I'm not who I used to be–"

"You *are*. You ain't change a bit. You even fixed my windows so they don't rattle anymore," Amos reminded him. "You're just scared of yourself. We're tryna change that so that you ain't anymore." Amos patted Mars' shoulder, "You need sleep. Let's go to bed. I already checked it this morning so you should be fine."

Mars shook his head, "I just need to die. How could I have sliced up Dao like that? Isaiah could've been hit, too–"

"Mars, dude, you're starting to go in circles again. We got another early day tomorrow so we can finish this record. You're getting a better handle on your shards, Isaiah is calming down–"

"You can't hear what I hear–"

"This is why we have mid-session meetings, Mars. So we can *talk* about it." Amos blindly searched Mars' left hand and plucked away the shard. It felt sharper than he remembered seeing. "We need to go to bed, both of us. Let's go."

Amos took Mars by the shoulder and guided him out of the kitchen into the living room. He threw away the shard into the tall kitchen trashcan as they passed. It landed quietly on spent paper towels spotted with Mars' blood from other outbursts earlier that week. The living room was luminated softly with a single lamp that stood over a reclined, chocolate brown comfy chair. The lamp shade was an old cymbal Amos brought to a shop to have made into the lamp that stood over his chair. The bronze lamp lit the room with a yellow-orange glow. The cousins walked through the living room, past the hung television and dark tan couch, and went up the stairs. Mars' head was hung low. Amos guided his footsteps.

The next morning, Isaiah showed up midday, just like Amos texted him late last night. Mars was sent to the market with a long list and Isaiah showed up with a paint-speckled bucket loaded with wall patching materials borrowed from his parents. Dressed in a worn grey plaid shirt and navy gym shorts, Isaiah rang Amos' brass doorbell. Within moments, he was greeted by a weary but smiling drummer.

"So glad you came," Amos said as he smoothed down his black, bleach-stained tank top and held open the door for the guitarist to walk through.

Waddling the heavy bucket in, Isaiah asked, "Where's the storm?"

Amos closed the door as he replied, "At the market. Eating me out of house and home."

Isaiah landed the bucket on the floor with a clatter. "You *trust* him to be with people? With*out* attempting to 'accidentally' kill someone? What if a siren rides past and he freaks out?"

Amos tried to wave off the concern, "He's not *that* bad. At least not that bad anymore. Mars gotta learn how to control his abilities when around people when by himself. Besides, he's got his headphones. They help block out other people's thoughts and keep him focused."

"How?" Isaiah asked.

"Megadeath, The Prodigy, Blindside and a *lot* of Marley," Amos replied. "If it can fill his head up, it's on the playlist. And isn't too negative. Please remind me to never *ever* let him listen to Deep Six Mafia for as long as I live, okay? I nearly needed a new basement and the plumber *still* thinks I busted the water heater myself. He also started listening to Jazz and Scott Joplin. They've been calming him down. He can even sleep to it. Tried TLC but it made him think of Danielle so that's off the list."

Isaiah was astonished. "The fact you don't slip tranqs into his food shocks me. Like, there's familia but this is above and *beyond*."

Amos shrugged, "Familia is important and Mars is familia–"

"Homicidal familia–"

"*Still* familia," Amos firmly reminded. "He wasn't always like this and you know that. He needs help. I'm gonna give it to him. What'd you bring?"

Isaiah ruffled through the bucket, showcasing some of what he brought, "I didn't know how bad Mars got and you didn't say much other than how Mars went off again so I got everything I brought from last time. Paint, spackle, spreaders and wall tape. And just to cover all bases, a couple furniture pens and some really strong glue. Oh – and a sewing kit for upholstery."

Amos chuckled, "Ice, you think of everything, don't you?"

Isaiah joked back, "Every band should have a kit for when one of their members goes Magneto. I think it was in the most recent issue from *Billboard*. Or maybe *Revolver* or *Kerrang*. I think 30 Seconds was on the cover or something."

Amos smiled, "It's just some small holes in the kitchen. Mars' dreads got sharp and darted the walls."

Isaiah stood up with a blank face. "He what? Dude, are you okay–"

"I'm fine, the holes are small and no one got hurt. Mars just had a moment, that's all," Amos assured. "You know how he gets sometime–"

"Yeah, and then the bassist needs a new *face*," Isaiah cocked back. "Amos, he's gonna *kill* you one day if you fool arou–"

"I ain't dead yet," Amos stated.

"*'Yet'*. Operative word," Isaiah said with his thumb and forefinger close.

"Mars doesn't have it in him–"

"How do you know? We ain't him, you're not in his head!"

"I knew him his whole life–"

"People *change*, Amos! Over little things, over big things. People *change*. Mars is different now! How you–"

"What do you suggest I do then?" Amos fumed.

"I don't know! I just don't know! But he may kill one of us! Already tried with Dao–"

Amos thundered, "That was *not* on purpose! You know that–"

"Still nearly happened! Amos, you gotta fix *holes in your walls* because your cousin has episodes where he gets mad and *glass* comes out of him. And this is at *least* once a week! Oh! And he can read your thoughts, because why the hell not? If we're gonna ride the weirdo train, might as well go full speed!" Isaiah was beside himself. He started raking through his hair and tugging on one of his curls.

Amos tried to calm himself and replied, "Look, Mars is a work in progress. Can we go patch my wall, please, por favor? Be*fore* 'the storm' returns and I have a new problem?"

Isaiah picked up the bucket and sighed with the heft of the weight, "Lead the way, Mr. Zavala. Isaiah Wall Patching Service at your … service – just show me the damage."

Amos showed Isaiah into the kitchen and presented the damage. Isaiah's jaw dropped from the drywall dust on the floor, the dark punctures and how a sizeable amount of them were head-level.

"Dude, he – he really *did* try to kill you!" Isaiah breathed.

Amos took the bucket from Isaiah and sat it down to fish out the plastic jar of spackle paste and metal spreaders, "No blood and I'm fine. This should be a quick, fifteen-minute patch up. In and out."

Isaiah opened the spackle jar and picked up a spreader. As he scooped out a small glob of chalk white paste onto the corner, he muttered, "Dao would *freak* if he saw this. He still gets nightmares about that day."

Amos heard Isaiah. "Maaaan, Dao ain't here. We are. I'm doin' all this so none of us will have to worry ever again, Dao included." The drummer dipped out a small glob on his spreader and smeared it over a lower hole on the wall. He scraped the spreader over the hole and in a couple swipes, it was gone, filled with paste that was a tone or two different from Amos' blanche walls.

"No, but he's still affected. You love Mars and that's great but Dao's got a burden to carry now." Isaiah filled in three close holes. Clean punctures, too. That means whatever Mars shot, it was fast and beyond sharp.

"Ice, Ice. *Please*," Amos pled irate. "I know. But I'm not gonna tie Mars up, throw him on a boat and sail him down the river or something in the middle of the night."

"No, because then he would be another town's problem that would miraculously float back to us." Isaiah put on his best newscaster voice as he filled in a few more holes, "Local singer kills ten, seven injured using what appears to be glass coming out of his skin. Five cops are in intensive care, band reports 'was not aware of rampage.' Guitarist and co-founder of band refused comments as he left quickly in a taxi. Label owner befuddled and enraged. Details at eleven, back to you, Mike."

Amos sniffed derisively, "That was very vivid."

Isaiah continued in his newscaster voice, "Drummer and co-founder Alvin 'Amos' Zavala – you know they'd mess up your last name, right? – states 'Mars is completely safe and harmless, he's my cousin.' Bassist Davis 'Dao' Milton claims local singer could pose harm to populace. 'My face wasn't always like this,' musician states. Drummer disagrees, details at eleven. Back to you, Suzie."

Amos rubbed the corner of his eye with the back of his wrist, "You are seriously trippin', man. Won't be like that. He's gonna be fine. The music is helping him focus and sleep and he's getting better and better. You don't see it during our practices?"

"What I see," Isaiah said in his normal voice, "is a struggling singer that got glass coming out of him and can't stop hearing everyone's thoughts about him. He thinks he's a monster, tries to act like one, too. He's frosted out less, yeah, but I have no idea if we're in a lull or when his bad moods will strike again. You know Mars, he don't like being caged in any way, shape or form. And that's *exactly* what you doin'." The guitarist tidied up a hole and got more spackle.

"I'm just working on his head, that's all. So he don't ever slip back, or at least not slip back as bad as he's gotten in the past." Amos scraped off the remainder of spackle on his spreader against the inner rim of the jar. "Are you done your section yet? I'm done down here."

Isaiah looked over his neat handiwork of covered holes, each were smoothly blended and filled. "Yeah, I'm done. Are you sure you wanna paint this over when it's dry? Why not wait until Mars leaves so you can just do it all in one go?"

Amos stood up and looked over his wall. From afar, it looked whole and complete again, the only signs of what happened that remained was the dust on the floor, filled with footprints. Amos' phone chimed, he received a text message. It was from Mars.

"Mars' gonna be back soon," Amos told Isaiah as he eyed his phone. "May wanna leave soon if you don't wanna see him."

Isaiah didn't miss a beat packing up his stuff, he threw everything into the bucket, "You ain't gotta tell me twice. Tell 'im I called and said 'Sup'."

"Sure," Amos agreed. He followed Isaiah to the front door and let the guitarist out. Amos closed the door and leaned against it. Isaiah was right, Mars could be a loose cannon. *What if his secret* did *get out?* Amos pondered. The very thought ran his blood cold. No one would understand, Amos was sure of that. *They'd probably shoot first, ask questions later. It would be such a massacre,* Amos worried. He was more concerned for the police that would have undoubtedly shown up than he was for his own cousin. Kevlar doesn't keep glass bullets or javelins out of heads. And given everything Amos had seen of Mars' abilities, the drummer figured his cousin could probably puncture body armor like paper if he was angry or scared enough. *That would* really *be the beginning of the end for all of us,* Amos worried as he went back into the kitchen to prepare lunch.

Everyday was an arduous struggle to get Mars to some sort of okay normalcy. At least enough to mitigate the bad days. However, there was considerable progress, Amos didn't have to call Isaiah as much for repairs, but Mars still had days where it was as if everything went back to week one. No matter what, Danielle still wanted her husband home.

One day, Danielle decided to give Amos a call. The day was a tad overcast but quite bright and there was a bit of chill in the air as the seasons shifted. She had just dropped the girls off at school and a wave of irritation passed over her. She was alone, she had no one to come home to, no one to tell her day to, no one to talk to. His absence was maddening and she could hardly take any more of it. And worst of all, Amos had banned her from seeing Mars for the past couple of weeks, said Mars wasn't doing too well.

Her rose-covered phone laid in her lap, the ringing resounded loud through the car's speaker. The car was a little new, only a couple years old, but already a litany of cartoon stickers took over a corner of the rear window. She waited at a stop light, looking around at the quiet intersection.

Amos answered brightly, "Hey, Dani–"

"Is Mars alright?" Danielle couldn't keep the worry out of her voice.

Amos tried to give his best answer, "Uhhh ... Mars – Mars is just nappin' now, he had a rough day."

"*Another* one?" Danielle was beside herself. "I'm coming over." The light changed and she started down a different road, away from home.

"Dani, don't!" Amos cautioned. "It–"

"Amos, I love what you're tryin' to do but that is my *husband* in your house!" she ripped. "It's like he's been on the road, I haven't seen him in so long but instead, he's *fifteen minutes away.* How long do you think this is gonna *last?*"

"Dani, I –"

"No excuses, Amos. I am *not* Savalez!" She knew every story Amos told, every web he had ever woven since the start. She wanted to protect her husband as much as he did but she was not about to be party to another one of his storytimes. She was sick of it.

And Amos knew it. He was rendered speechless. Never has Danielle ever been quick to anger but Amos could tell she certainly had enough. He could see it in her texts, hear it lurking behind her tone during their calls. She was through and another lie was not going to be the balm that saves him. Even the longest candles burn down.

"Nothing, Amos?" Danielle dared. "Then I'll be seeing my husband, then. Mars needs me." She knew she was roughly seven minutes away and sped a bit to make it quicker.

"Dani, he may slide back if he sees you!" Amos warned.

Danielle was floored, "*How?*"

Amos had little to rebut with. Mars asked for her every night, even on the worst ones. If he didn't ask for her, he talked about her. It took little time for Amos to discover Danielle was a wonderful carrot to inspire Mars to get better but it was a bit of a tricky carrot, for it was also a strong switch to trigger his guilt and dark episodes. And dark episodes *always* became destructive episodes. There were countless nights where Amos consoled Mars over being away from his family. They either ended with a pat on the back or another text to Isaiah.

Though his mental gag bag was empty, that didn't stop Amos from trying. "He ... he may be a bit out of sorts when you see him," Amos offered weakly.

Danielle laughed off such a foolish notion. "Do you know how *long* I have *known* Mars? He has only spent fourteen – maybe sixteen years on this planet with*out* me. I have seen *every*thing. From when he fell at Junior prom in front of the school, to when Savalez wouldn't stop yankin' you all about with weird promises on the first album, to when we passed all of you on the cover of a magazine about your second gold record as we walked to the food bank together because there wasn't enough to feed *any. Of. Us.* I'm seeing my husband, Amos. If he's out of whack, it's because I'm not there. Mars *needs me.* The girls ask for him every night. Every. *Night.*" She curved around a corner sharply. She made amazing time, just a couple minutes away.

Amos had nothing worthwhile to refute. She was stubborn, just like Mars. And she was also right. Amos just hoped his house would hold up. The plumber had already blacklisted him, they were *not* interested in "goin' behind rock stars after they trash their houses. Ain't do it for Bowie. Ain't do it for Ozzy. Not gonna do it for you. No money in the world is good enough for putting up with this." Amos was sure there was more in that email the plumber sent but that paragraph and the bill was more than enough.

"I'll see you when you get here, Dani," said a weakly resigned Amos before he hung up.

Almost a minute and a half later, Danielle was at the door. She didn't bother to ring the brass doorbell or knock.

Instead she fished out the spare key Amos trusted her with out of her topaz bomber jacket and opened the door.

Amos rushed to the door from the kitchen, unready and blithering excuses.

Danielle wanted to hear none of it. "Where is Mars?" she demanded with a slight tinge of familial kindness that was definitely not present on her irritated face. She waited for him to tumble out some more excuses.

"He's sleep upstai – Dani, wait!" Amos hurried up the stairs behind his cousin-in-law after he closed the front door. "He's still sleep!"

Danielle continued storming up the stairs. She saw the wide open door of Amos' bedroom and walked in. Before her laid her husband in Amos' king-sized bed. A woven umber blanket sat folded at the foot of the bed. He still had on his day clothes, a brown shirt and denim shorts. His hair was tightly braided and some dreads glinted with a thin coat of glass. His face was pained, his body a little curled up. Odd music played from the bluetooth speaker on the bed beside the pillow, ragtime and bird noises overlapped.

Mars shivered, horned glass grew from his shoulder and then receded back slowly like a wave. Danielle started towards the bed but Amos stopped her.

He whispered harshly, "What are you *doing?*"

She responded in rapid Dominican Spanish, "He's cold! I'm gonna put a blanket over him!"

"Let me do it–"

"*Why?*" Danielle shot in English.

Amos shrugged, "He could wake up–"

Danielle shoved past Amos and grabbed the blanket. She drew it over Mars lovingly. Amos merely watched, hopeful Mars wouldn't wake up or, worse, hurt Danielle.

Mars stirred as Danielle smoothed the blanket over him. She laid a gentle hand upon Mars' head and smiled. Amos' stomach dropped.

"What are you *doing?*" Amos strained.

Danielle ignored him and bent over to kiss Mars on his temple. She did this always when he was sick, just as he did when she was sick.

Mars' eyes fluttered open. He almost couldn't believe what he saw before him. Mars paused as he looked at her, he couldn't figure out if he was still dreaming.

"Dani?" Mars asked bleary tongued.

"Hey, sleepyhead," Danielle beamed as she rubbed Mars' head. It was like old times. Her heart bloomed with such love for her husband. Married for eleven years but known him for thirteen, Danielle never tired of his face or the comfort he made her feel. No one loved her more than him and she felt the same.

Mars' skin moved under her hand. Danielle hesitated for a moment but continued to rub his head again.

He's tryin' to get better, Mars heard Danielle think. He also heard the frantic thoughts of Amos: *Mars, please be good. Please don't do anything stupid. Just be a happy Mars. Make her think you're getting better.*

Mars tried to blink the thoughts away. He asked Danielle, "Have you been here long?"

Danielle shook her head, "No. Just got here. How're you

feeling?"

"How about the girls?" Mars asked.

He avoided the question, Danielle mentally noted.

"I'm doin' okay," Mars rushed out. "Just – I think about you guys every day. I wish I were home."

"Me too," Danielle agreed. She asked Amos, "When *can* I have my husband back?" Danielle sat on the side of the bed, Mars sought out her hand and held it. His hand lightly ruptured but quickly quelled. She rubbed his hand.

Amos tried to shake off his anxiety. "He's – he's been doin' good but – but he still a work in progress. I wanna make sure he don't have to come back. I'd say a few weeks. Like, three."

Danielle nodded with kind approval, "I hope it will be sooner. Mars, the girls ask for you every day."

Mars smiled, "I ask Amos for you all every day, too."

Amos cleared his throat. "You're getting better every day, Mars. I just want everyone to see you at your *absolute* best. Dani, can Mars sleep? He had a tiring day."

Danielle kissed Mars' hand and asked, "Did you? Are you okay?"

Mars answered, "It was nothin', Dani. I just had a weird mornin–"

"'Weird', how?" Danielle inquired.

Amos hurried over, "He had more shards show up–"

Danielle halted Amos, "Amos, *please.*" She turned back to her husband and asked with care, "Honey, how?"

Mars replied, "What Amos said. I just needed rest. I promise."

Danielle raised off the bed and kissed Mars' hand again. "I'll let you sleep, then." She kissed his temple.

Amos offered, "I got some tea goin' downstairs. You can go down and I'll catch up, I just wanna make sure Mars is doin' fine."

Danielle eyed Amos suspiciously but reluctantly agreed, "Fine then. Just don't take too long, Mars gotta sleep." She left out, closing the door behind her.

Amos pulled in close to Mars, "How you feelin', man? Any shards?"

Mars' face turned stormy, "I just ... I couldn't tell her–"

"You don't have to–"

"I was *so* close. So close to killing myself. Why'd you dilute the cleaning stuff under the sink?" Tears collected in Mars' eyes.

Amos patted Mars' shoulder, "Thinking ahead. Just sleep and it'll be fine. Just stay in *bed*. You puked a *lot*. Just chill and sleep. Try not to think about it. I'll take care of Dani, just sleep, cuz." Amos patted Mars' side, "Try to sleep it off."

Mars sniffed, "She needs someone less crazy." He frowned and threw his hands over his eyes. He croaked, "She deserves so much better. So much better."

Amos pursed his lips. "You'll get better, I promise. You get a little better every day. Just sleep and stay in bed. I'm gonna give you some time to, y'know, handle your feelings but you need to rest."

Mars nodded from underneath his hands. He then whimpered out a quiet sob.

Amos turned away and left the room. It broke his heart seeing Mars this way.

Downstairs, he found at the kitchen table three cups of tea, one with a small plate over it. Danielle sat at the table, blowing on her cup.

"Mars is getting better, y'know." Amos said as he sat down. He picked up his cup of tea and blew on it himself. It was sweet and with a mellow flowery scent. He could tell she added extra honey and most likely did the same for Mars' cup.

"Did you really mean 'three weeks'?" Danielle asked.

Amos nodded as he sipped. "Mm-hm, he's controlling the glass so much better now. We're just smoothing the edges."

Danielle sighed and looked at the covered cup. "He doesn't deserve this. Mars is a *good* man. Not a day go by that I don't wonder what we did to deserve this?"

Amos replied, "Stuff happens. That's life. All we can do is just be there for Mars and help him. If he's surrounded by love–"

"But what about Dao? And Isaiah? Dao especially. He looked so bad in that hospital. He didn't deserve it either." Danielle sniffed. "I wish we could all go back to the way things used to be. Before all of this." Danielle could never forget Dao's terrified, uncertain face as the doctors rushed him off the ambulance. Neither could she forget Mars' frantic behavior, she had never seen him act like that. It was something more than guilt, much more.

"I know how you feel," Amos admitted. "When I saw Dao get struck, for a moment, I thought he was dead. Mars freaked out so bad. He wanted *no* one to come near him. I thought he'd run outside and start screamin' at the traffic or somethin' wild. Now, Dao's face is messed up and Mars' head is messed up. Isaiah is just tryin' to keep us together but I know he be wonderin' when he's next. So many pieces to pick up. Too many pieces." Amos drank more tea. "I … My biggest fear … I just wanna make sure I never get a call about the girls or you getting the same fate. I … I just wouldn't – I couldn't live with myself."

Danielle sighed. Her cup warmed her hand as she gazed back at herself in the tea's golden reflection. Her cup smelled mellow but was much less sweet. She looked at Amos, "Amos, we're not hapless, helpless–"

"Neither is Dao. It's just, when Mars hits, he's quick like a viper. One second fine, next second, mayhem." Amos rubbed his neck, "I know you want Mars back. I do too, it's like we ten again, livin' under the same roof. But I wanna be one-hundred and fifty percent *sure* ain't nothin' bad gon' happen. I already got Dao on my conscious, I don't need to add more weight."

"Amos, we're here for you, okay?" Danielle offered. "I just want Mars to be okay. I miss him. So do the girls."

"I know," Amos replied.

That night, it was dinnertime at the Juarez house. The girls sat at the table with their mother, eating their egg salad sandwiches and sharing their day. The television played on in the background, a colorful cartoon with the sound turned down low.

Vivica was loudest and proudest, "The teacher got our class a fishy today!" She couldn't contain her excitement as she bounced in her chair.

Violet was enchanted by the news, "Ooooh, what color is it?"

"It's black and purple with flowy fins!" Vivica declared. "It has a big tank! Mommy! Can Daddy make a prettier place for the fishy to live?"

Danielle replied, "I'll ask Daddy if he can."

Violet asked her mother, "Mama, when Daddy gonna come back? Is he on tour again?"

Vivica answered, "I thought he was at Uncle Amos's house?"

Danielle tried to smile at the questions. She knew they were sincere but they hurt all the same. "Uncle Amos said three weeks, then Daddy will be back."

"Why is Daddy away for so long?" Violet asked.

Danielle replied the best answer she could, "The glass makes him a little sick sometimes. He was very sick when he got his ... powers." The word sounded so odd but she went with it anyways. "He needed to feel better and Uncle Amos is helping him get better. Now, he's only a *little* sick and will be back soon."

Vivica pondered, "Does it hurt his tummy? He would cough sometimes and it would sound a little bad."

Danielle frowned a bit, "You could hear his coughs sometimes?"

"Yah," Vivica replied. Violet nodded with her as she continued, "I think the glass gives him really bad colds."

"A little bit," Danielle said. "He just has to focus on getting better so when he comes back, he won't cough or have tummy-aches anymore." Danielle felt awful that she had to lie to her children but they didn't need to know the truth: sometimes Mars coughed because he would try to swallow his glass shards whenever he thought no one was around or paying attention. She had caught him in the act at least twice but the results were usually the same, incessant coughing. Though what alarmed her most was that Amos told her that he's seen worse.

In effort to change the subject, Danielle suggested, "Hey, how about we watch a movie together and order pizza?"

The girls erupted in their seats, thrilled. Danielle tried to smile. *I hope Amos knows what he's doing – but I hope he keeps his word, most of all,* she thought.

1.3

The holidays had rolled around. Mars was still at Amos' house, irritated and quick to temper. Three weeks had come and gone but Mars "still wasn't safe enough". Not a day went by that Mars didn't express his disdain one way or another. Amos would find parts of his bed or doors with slashes in them regularly. Once, the bathroom mirror cracked loudly as Amos brushed his teeth and spiked out a bit before it healed itself perfectly again. Amos then had heard footsteps outside resume walking down the hall. It wasn't the greatest idea Amos could have come up with but it was the best one to save the band and his cousin at the same time. It wasn't just Mars in need: Isaiah was still frightened of Mars taking his tahm off. And Dao still had trauma from what happened to him.

Danielle was worse. She came on the last day of the third week, ready to take Mars home. When Amos broke the news, she was a blistering rage of fury. She would have probably dragged Mars out herself if she didn't watch the television and couch glass over and hear Mars cough violently upstairs. The chaos that ensued between Danielle and Amos caused Mars to have another episode. Another glass swallowing attempt. Danielle reluctantly agreed to another month, four in total.

To appease Mars, Amos decided to have Christmas at his house. Something cheery for everyone. Just the five of them; Mars, Amos, Danielle and the girls.

"Maaaaaaars!" Amos called out as he stirred soup on the stove, "You ready? Dani and the girls are gonna be here any min–"

Mars glided down the stairs and into the kitchen on a thick sheet of glass. It faded into the ground as he stepped off, he brimmed with quiet eagerness. His hair was folded into a neat braid and a glass bauble at the end. He had on a plain shirt and dark pants, he was never much for holiday wear. But he definitely couldn't wait to see his wife and daughters again.

Stunned at the entrance, Amos quipped, "That's new. Doing a Silver Surfer thing now, that's cool. Remember–"

"I'll be a good boy," said Mars. He tried to not let Amos' rules sour his mood today.

"Just sayin', bro. This morning was a little touch-and-go–"

"Then put me down already and be done with it–"

Amos shook his head, "Mars, *pleas*–"

There was a tight rap on the door. Danielle and the girls were here.

"*Try* to be cheery?" Amos urged quietly before he went to grab the door.

Danielle and the girls wore bright smiles and colorful reindeer clothing. Danielle carried a couple bags in tow, filled with presents. The girls' hair were done up in adorable puffy twists and barrettes shaped like holiday bulbs.

Amos greeted them warmly, "Hey, hey! Feliz Navidad! Te amo, te amo, te *amo!*" He picked up the girls, "Ohhhhh! Both of you are getting *big!*"

"Anyone miss me?" asked Mars from the kitchen. His fear of himself kept him riveted to the spot. Fear of what he could do to his daughters, what he did to Dao–

"Daddy!" both girls exclaimed. They clambered out of Amos' arms and sprinted to their father. Oh, how glad they were to see him, it had been so long. Mars crouched down to accept their love, he missed it dearly. He could hear their thoughts of joy, love and wonder; they warmed his heart.

Vivica asked first, "Daddy, are you okay yet?"

"When are you coming home?" Violet followed up.

Mars looked to Amos. "Hey, when *am* I coming home?" His voice held charm but with a light dart underneath.

Amos glanced at Danielle and back to Mars, rubbing his neck, "Should be soon–"

"Tonight?" asked Mars with a pleasant smile.

"Ma-maybe," Amos stammered, put on the spot. "Probably tomorrow morning if your … if you don't get sick tonight."

The girls cheered and hugged their father. Vivica burrowed herself into his chest, Violet wrapped her arms around his neck. Mars kissed them both.

"You both look so beautiful today," Mars complemented in Spanish.

Danielle came into the kitchen, heart swollen with joy. "They couldn't wait to see you." She hugged him as well.

Amos cherished the moment. This was why he worked so hard. Mars was like his old self again, happy and full of life. Amos took this moment to give his decorations a once over. The tree looked magnificent, glittered with colorful baubles, tinsel and glass frost. Amos woke up to the glass frost that morning. He thought it was fine until he found Mars trying to choke on one of the needles. Mars' body rejected it with a rounded capsule of glass.

The wreaths and boughs looked lovely, Slice gave them to him through Isaiah. Amos could tell that Slice was driving Dao up a wall with his care. Countless times he had heard Dao exclaim to his brother, "I'm not blind in *both* eyes!"

Amos returned to his family and clapped, "Who wants apple cider and candy?"

The girls jumped around their father like hungry chicks, "I do! I do!"

The day was quite normal, all things considering. Mars was his normal self, playing with the girls, tossing jokes – not hidden jabs – at Amos, dragging his wife onto his lap for quick holiday pictures.

Then the doorbell rang.

"Can't we just leave the gifts on the steps and leave?" suggested Dao. "Like, 'ding dong ditch' but with presents?"

"Because Mars would know and – hiiiii, Amos!" Isaiah tried to be quiet but was startled by Amos opening the door.

He was expecting Mars. Loud and robotic from the shock, he greeted, "Fe-liz Na-vi-dad!"

Amos spotted the bag of gifts hung from Dao's fingers. His jacket was better suited for the weather. He was still hunched over and had a popped collar to hide his scars. Isaiah simply wore a long, knitted scarf, a tank top and paint splattered pants. *Probably thinking ahead*, Amos thought.

"Feliz Navidad!" Amos replied as he welcomed Dao and Isaiah in. "Everyone, Dao and Isaiah dropped by!"

The moment Dao and Isaiah spotted Mars on the couch watching television with his head laid upon Danielle's shoulder, Mars perked up from the flurry of panicked thoughts that struck him. He had already known Isaiah and Dao were coming, he could hear them ponder contingency plans when they were back in the car. That and Dao's muffler was starting to go bad. But now, their thoughts were like a rife tsunami of words.

"Hey," said Mars, "could you guys keep it down a little?" He snuggled back onto Danielle's shoulder, "I want to hear this."

Dao and Isaiah were mum. Amos clapped them both on the shoulder and spoke quietly between them, "Food's in the kitchen, come get some." The three traveled into the kitchen.

Low voiced, Dao asked, "How's he been all day?" The men had huddled in close by the stove, the furthest point in the kitchen and the house.

Amos shrugged and wobbled his hand, "Ehhh, so-so. Not so hot this morning but been great all this afternoon. He really wants to go home, back to Dani and the girls. Just let him stay glued to her and we'll all have a happy Christmas."

Isaiah was astonished, "That's all we needed? Just Dani to show up and he's a bunny?"

Amos faltered a quick, quiet laugh. "No tellin'. Probably keeping a tight lid because the girls are here." He shrugged, "Who knows what will come later. Just get some food and I'll put the presents out with the others."

As Dao handed over the bag, Isaiah asked, "Wait, you don't open presents in the morning on Christmas?"

"Mars," Amos summed up.

"Ah," noted Isaiah. He was sorry that he asked.

Dao and Isaiah worked on fixing themselves food from the stove as Amos headed out. The menu was meager this year in comparison to all the others. Amos was a very capable cook but with Mars to look after, a leaner menu meant less glass checks. More soups, easy to strain through. No empanadas, too easy to hide glass. The turkey was enormous and roasting, hopefully too dense to hide glass in. The gravy was thin and watery, almost no rice side dishes, absent stuffing. Isaiah and Dao had hoped for a banquet.

"Amos should have just settled for pizza, fries and wings," muttered Dao.

"Dao eats meat now?" Isaiah joked.

"Just thinkin' 'bout everyone," replied Dao.

In the living room, Amos kneeled by the tree and laid out new presents. The girls were curled up in front of the TV, fast asleep.

Danielle said to Mars, "More presents? Wow, won't the

girls be excited?" She had been thoroughly charmed by Mars all day. He was like his old self again – funny, sweet and happy. She was a little hesitant at first to let Mars touch her so freely but his wit and her disdain for the distance between them warmed her quick. But his tired eyes told her none of this came with ease.

Amos chuckled, "I know, right? Good year."

Dao and Isaiah came out, filled plates in hand. They would usually plop down on the couch next to Mars but instead they looked for anywhere else to sit. But unfortunately, there wasn't anywhere else.

Isaiah suggested, "Dao, you wanna be in the dining room? It would suck if we got food on the floor."

Dao nodded, "Yeah, let's go."

The duo left for the dining room. It was decorated with hung hollies and glass icicles. Dao and Isaiah paused at the icicles. They receded away. As they tried to sit in any seat not near a window or glass door cupboard, they heard Mars call out, "Maybe we should open our presents. It couldn't happen this morning so why not now?"

Isaiah and Dao froze again.

Before either the guitarist or the bassist could drum up any excuse, Amos agreed, "Maybe that's a good idea. I'll go wake the girls up."

Amos went over and started rocking the girls awake. They started to stir with whines. Amos whispered to each of them, "Time for presents. Come on, time for presents." They rose a little quicker.

Meanwhile, Isaiah and Dao rose out of their chairs and trudged back into the living room. The tree was next to the couch, beside Danielle and Mars. They waited for Amos to hand out the presents. Mars was like a hungry lion to Dao and Isaiah, they did everything they could to not get close.

Bundles of presents crowded in Amos' lap, where he sorted them by name. As he did, Mars took his wife's hand and laid his hand over her wrist. Around it formed a glass cuff bracelet, it glinted like a million diamonds in the tree lights. Inscribed inside were clear letters that read "Dani Cali, My Only Love".

Danielle was shocked. The cuff was beautiful and the words touching … but she instinctively feared for something worse to happen. She still had dreams about the day he almost sliced her throat and hips.

She stammered, "It – it's lov-lovely–"

"Is it not pretty enough? Too heavy?" asked Mars. He wanted her to like it. He wanted to try and show that he cared, that the old Mars was still there somewhere. That he wanted to be home, with her.

Amos looked up at Danielle's rattling voice, Dao and Isaiah were riveted to the spot. The girls rummaged through the presents still under the tree.

"Hey, girls," Amos said quietly, "I gotta chat with daddy for a sec. If you need anything, ask Mommy, or Uncle Dao and Uncle Isaiah, okay?"

"Okay!" both girls cheered before ripping through their gifts.

Amos beckoned Mars upstairs, "Mars? Uno momento,

por favor? Just gonna be quick."

Mars glowered at Amos for a moment before he switched to a kinder face to kiss his wife. "I'll be back," he promised her.

Amos leading the way, Mars headed up the stairs into Amos' room. Mars closed the bedroom door behind them with a small wave of glass rippling out the floor.

"Amos," Mars snarled, "I've been *good* all day–"

"What happened down there? Why'd Dani sound–"

"I surprised her–"

"'Surprised' sounded like 'scared' to me–"

Mars' dreads rose, covered with a thin plate of glass. "Do *not* keep her from me. She is not hurt, I gave her a bracelet. Let me have this one moment of normalcy. *Please.*"

Amos wanted to back away but kept steady, "Mars, please don't start. Pleas–"

"Then why am I up here?" Mars' skin rumbled.

"To check on you, man!" Amos strained to keep his voice low. "I want you to be able to go home today. To be with Dani and the girls! But I can't do that if I'm looking up and I see her with a worried face on. That's why I'm checking."

Mars skin smoothed and his dreads lowered. He got on his knees and said, "Amos, leave me be or kill me already." A glass dagger materialized beside Mars. "I don't want to live anymore, you know that–"

"Ohhhh, please don't start," Amos begged, irritated. Mars was sliding back and fast. Just when things were cheery.

Mars offered the dagger, "Then finish me. It'll be easy, I won't scream, I won't struggle–"

"I'm trying to keep you from doing this at home with Dani and the kids!" Amos could barely keep a lid on his temper and his volume. "Dani's caught you choking on shards! That means the girls could spot you–"

"Mars?" Danielle called up the stairs. "Mars? Is everything fine?"

Quietly, Mars said to Amos, "Dani's worrying about me. I can hear it in her head. She wants me to come home. She wants me to be okay. If you won't kill me, then, please–" the dagger receded into his hand "–let me be."

Mars got up and left, he pulled the door shut behind him.

In adoring Spanish, Amos heard Mars assure her, "I'm fine, I'm fine. Last minute checkup from Dr. Amos. Does everyone love their presents?"

Amos left his room, he found Danielle wrapped in Mars' arms at the bottom of the stairs, smiling. He wondered how much of her grin was real and how much was a placating front. He could hear Dao and Isaiah playing with the girls and marveling over the gifts. Amos sighed.

"Mars, the girls love the dolls you bought them," said Danielle as Mars nuzzled her. "And the bracelet is beautiful. I was just a little shocked–"

"I know," said Mars in English. "I didn't mean to spook you."

"Maaaaaaaaaaaaaaa!" Vivica shouted, thrilled from all her gifts. "Why does the bracelet say 'Dani Cali'?"

Danielle and Mars chuckled. Amos came down the stairs, a bright smile plastered on his face for the girls, and went over to sit with Dao and Isaiah. They sat on the floor in front of the tree, he sat on the couch. Amos hoped the couch was safe, he was too weary to check.

"'Dani Cali' is the nickname your father gave me when we met," explained Danielle.

Dao snickered, "Tryna be slick, right, Ice?"

Isaiah shrugged with a little smile, "It worked, obviously."

Violet chirped at her sister, "Uncle Dao said we could have the ice cream when Daddy came back! Let's go!"

Before anyone could say anything, the girls darted into the kitchen and scrambled to pull out a chair and assemble to open the freezer. What they discovered was a giant tub of butter brickle ice cream. The girls were over the moon at their find.

Though stunned by the speed of their dedicated fury, Amos gestured for no one to stop them. He tried to ease the moment instead.

"Ice, remember our first studio?"

Isaiah moaned with a wider smile, "Please tell me you aren't talkin' 'bout Doze!" When Amos busted into laughter, Isaiah waved, "C'mon, man! I was duty bound to secure us the spot! It was three months! Shortest relationship ever! Don't remind me."

Dao joked, "I really thought you liked him. He didn't seem too bad. Kept shovin' roses in your guitar when you weren't around–"

"I liked the *studio*, not Doze. Free recording, puppy dog producer, free food. Can't beat that. I never said I liked *him*." Isaiah slipped out a small chortle, "His sister was hot, though. Should have went out with her instead."

The guys laughed. Mars stopped after Danielle gave him a light pat on the shoulder.

Amos couldn't stop laughing, "'Ey, Isaiah, what you say when Mars found out and asked when you were going to make up your mind about guys and girls?"

Isaiah pumped his fists and mock yelled, "'*Never!*' Ha ha, I still haven't changed a bit. I'm one of the few constants …" Isaiah trailed off, realizing his words, "… of the … the band… erm, hey, uh … cool gift you got me, Amos. A – a pick holder with a spring in it that I can keep on my mic stand. Hope- hopefully I can keep them all in one place now when we tour."

Dao handed Amos his and Mars' gifts. Danielle retrieved Mars' gift and handed it to her husband. He opened the present carefully, it was wrapped tight. Soft and plush, the wrapping paper crinkled with his every touch. It was a speaker pillow.

"From Dao and I," said Isaiah. He hoped Mars liked it. At least well enough to not guillotine him in private.

Mars turned the pillow over and over, he didn't know how to feel. "Thank you," he said, "I appreciate this."

Amos opened his gift, it was a shirt that featured Aztec prints and pan-African colors. The left back hem read "Black Chicano Pride". Amos was touched.

Dao nudged Isaiah, "Told you he'd love it."

"Is the size good?" asked Isaiah.

Amos nodded. He checked the tag, "Fits me fine."

Night fell. Amos' house was quiet. Danielle and the girls slept in the basement, as per Amos' rules. Dao and Isaiah left hours ago, they had other households to visit (with bigger menus). Mars rested in his room next to Amos'. The day turned out well. No one died, no one had to be rushed to the hospital for "knife accidents", Christmas was a success.

But Mars had to stay. Danielle's suggestion. She loved him dearly and wanted him home more than anything but the shock of the bangle scared her. She didn't want to trip Mars into another episode in her adjustment. When she told Mars this in Amos' room, sitting on the bed with Mars as Amos supervised, Mars became completely undone. Danielle tried to soothe him the best she could but his skin wouldn't stop rippling.

"Mars, Mars, only for two weeks," Danielle assured. She wanted to touch his face and calm his tears but she hesitated. "I'm *definitely* having you home by Valentines'. Well before that." She tried to smile but her loving grin was weak. "You're getting *better*. I can see that. But ... I ... I still love you but I need to adjust, too."

Mars sank into her, defeated. His skin rumbled in patches of violent surge. Amos mouthed to Danielle if she needed help but she shook her head.

Danielle continued, "I want to make sure that when

you're home, everything will be fine. Everything. I'm going to visit you four times a week from now on, even bring the girls at least once a week."

Amos bartered, "Maybe three–"

Danielle cut him off with an icy glare. She kissed Mars' temple. His skin still moved and shifted in her arms. It quickened her heart but she still held firm. At least enough to calm her husband. "We will be there for you, Mars. I'm not going anywhere. Once all this adjusting is over, you'll be home soon enough. Amos has done such a great job with you, I just want to make sure it stays that way."

Mars squeezed her tight. Horned glass came out of the walls but they quickly receded. He didn't want anyone to use that as justification to tack on more time.

"I need you," croaked Mars. "I need you more than *anything*. Please let me come home tonight. I promise … I … I promise …" He didn't want to lie to her, he didn't want to say that he would be immediately better and all the sad days and episodes were behind him.

"Promise me you'll keep getting better so we can have you home sooner."

Mars kissed Danielle on the cheek. "Anything. Anything for you."

She patted his shoulder, "I know. I know." She felt his skin calm.

Then everyone made their way to bed. Danielle left for the basement, and Amos took Mars to his room. Amos was so tuckered out from his day that he forgot to check Mars' room. It was small and practically empty but that never stopped Mars. It dawned on Amos what he forgot as he drifted off to sleep.

When Amos checked on Mars, he found a small glass figurine on the nightstand. It was of Mars and Danielle, happy and smiling. The detail was impeccable and breathtaking, Amos was captivated. Then Mars stirred and off popped the head of the little glass figure of Mars. The head tinkered onto the nightstand with a gentle ring and a saddened face. It mouthed, "Please kill me." Amos turned away and left.

1.4

It was at a label meeting where the fruits of their labor paid off.

Delirium Shack Records was a small house of a business between a community center and a laundromat in Chula Vista. Standing for about fifteen years, they grew a fairly healthy stable of Rock, Ska and Punk acts. Within their red, graffitied halls were portraits of their best acts. At the entrance on the left was The Dowry Effect, the all-girl Punk band led by Deborah Willis – her half blue, half pink afro swirling as she yelled into a mic while her band played on behind her vibrantly. On the right was Lumination Rising, the four men stood stoic and upright, shoulder to shoulder. Dao was tallest, Amos was shortest but only by a hair to Mars and Isaiah. Beyond the two large portraits were show pictures of Delirium's comparatively smaller acts.

The men of Lumination Rising sat opposite of Rick Savalez, the label's owner, in a small, stuffy conference room. The window was open and the ceiling fan at steady rotation but all it did was just move the heat around. It was like this year-round, to the point everyone started calling the room "The Hot Seat", fitting for the label discussions that occurred there.

Savalez was nearing his fifties but still loved the music. Originally a fan when Thrash and Punk started hitting the West Coast, Savalez worked his way up from promoter to tour manager to head of his own small label. He saw what the genres could provide but also who was first to get pushed out of the scene as it grew more shine. He saw it with Blues, he saw it with Jazz. Even both Rap and Hip Hop were having a bleach problem. This made Savalez more determined but he also ran a tight ship to avoid feeling like he was picking up major labels' bad habits. He believed in family and that's how he saw his bands and employees. Even if it didn't feel that way at times.

He listened to a few demos from *Throwing Stones*, the hard-hitting cymbals and howl of fuzz guitar complemented the striking and staccato bass lines under the wild yell of vocals. After the last song "Hunting the Lies" faded out on Savalez's beaten up smartphone, the exec quieted the device. The room was silent, only the gentle buzz of the ceiling fan and traffic outside. Spring had just started but it still felt like an awful summer in the conference room.

The band sat with rapt attention. Mars' dreads were pulled back into a neat bun. Amos wrangled his navy baseball cap in his lap. Dao still covered half his face. Isaiah pulled on one of his curls.

"So ...," Savalez drawled, "When am I going to get the

rest of this?" He looked at each of the men before him, drumming his sausage fingers.

Amos spoke up, "It should be in by the end of this month."

Isaiah joined, "We're just cleaning up the last couple of songs."

Savalez looked up at the ceiling with a sigh and stared out the window, over the rooftops of Chula Vista. Looking back at the band, he asked, "Are you *sure* you don't need a producer? I got ChicoMadness–"

"We're *fine*," Amos countered. "You'll get your songs." He never liked when the label suggested additional people to come in. Savalez called it "spreading the pie", Amos saw it as others coming in to eat Lumination Rising's proper slices.

"Really?" Savalez snorted. "No other accidents? We can't keep Lumination if you guys *stay* in the hospital." He turned his attention to Mars and Dao. "How you two doin'? Mars? Dao?"

Dao looked at his bandmates and gazed at his clasped hands. "I'm good," he reported quietly. "My eye still can see a bit."

Savalez asked, "Dao, let me see your face."

The bassist hesitated at first but at Savalez's further prodding, Dao swept back his dreads. It was the first time he showed his full face to anyone outside of doctors, bandmates and family.

"Madre *Maria*, look at you," Savalez breathed as he winced away from Dao's deep scars and clouded right eye. Savalez waved at Dao blindly, "Put it away. Away!"

Dao parted his dreads with a quick swipe of a finger and covered half his face again.

Savalez looked at Mars, stunned. "Mars! You did all this? Dao looks like he was whipped halfway across the face with a hot chain!"

Mars sat silent.

"Mars!" Savalez pounded his fist on the granite top with a fierce thump, as if he tried to break it.

Mars turned away and looked out the window. His voice was soft, he didn't know what to say. "I...," the words could hardly escape him. He looked down at the table, staring at his reflection. With a little more resolve, Mars answered, "It was an accident."

"Accident or not, Mars! These things can't happen!" Savalez's roar filled the room.

"Rick," Amos interjected, "the band has already been through this. Mars still feels bad about this and he's heard it from all of us–"

"He hasn't heard it from *me*," Savalez slammed. "Mars, you got super lucky with your accident–" Mars attention was pulled to Savalez's words "–But Dao didn't get off so lucky. Fans are gonna *freak* when they see him."

Amos could sense Mars bristling. The drummer tried to change the subject, "Can we talk touring and release dates?"

Savalez wasn't done. He jutted an angry hand out at Dao and screamed, "How can I when your bassist looks like *this*!"

Dao muttered, irate, "I can still *play*."

Savalez caught Dao's utterance. "Good thing, too!" he shot back, "But no one is gonna be prepared to *see* you like this. Isaiah dying his hair silver – fine. Mars having dreads to the floor – fine. Your cuts? Have you *seen* yourself?"

"Every. *Day,*" Dao growled. "This is me, now. Take it or leave it."

Savalez slammed his hands on the table in exasperation. "I wanna leave it but I gotta *take* it!"

Before Dao could respond, there was a heavy pound at the door.

"Who is it?" Savalez yelled.

"Police!" A woman's husky voice roared. It was familiar: Deborah Willis. She cracked open the door and poked her head in. A lot gentler and without husk, she asked, "Can we come in, yet? Loco's 'bout to put your boy Chico in the hospital." She looked at Lumination Rising with a pitying smile, "And it seems like you already got enough of that–"

There was a small crash outside. Deborah looked back out behind her. Her drummer had an unlaced boot on the wall and a polo shirt-wearing producer in a full headlock. He was gagging and tapping at her arm in slaps. The Dowry Effect's bassist and guitarist couldn't help but to laugh and jeer at the producer.

Deborah looked back in the room. "We should really get in here," she smiled sweetly over the gagging noises.

Disturbed, Savalez roared, "Dowry! In here, *now.* Loco! Let him go!"

Though of small frame, Deborah was louder than Savalez. The Punk vocalist shouted to her band, "Tribe! Fall out and line up. Loco! Kick his ass later!"

One by one, the four members of The Dowry Effect

piled into the room, crowding it to standing room only. The drummer was the last to enter, she flipped off the producer as he laid on the ground, rasping for breath.

"Call me 'pendeja' one more time!" Loco dared vociferously as she stood in the doorway. "I'll tell everyone you steal beats!" She slammed the conference room door shut.

"Loco!" Savalez screamed.

Her light brown shoulders hitched in frozen surprise. She turned on a heel, still as a statue. "Sorry," the drummer meekly apologized. She slid behind Deborah in playful concern and draped an athletic toned arm over Deborah's shoulder, her forearm showed a typeset tattoo that read "Zapatista" vertically.

Dowry's bassist, Nakia Leah, sat on the cabinets beside the door. She wore a distressed military shirt that bore stenciled words: "Be a good mother: Abort misogyny". The guitarist, Lux, propped herself against the wall. Tattoos lined her neck and down her dark arms.

Savalez drew in a deep breath and exhaled tiredly, "Loco, why did you put Chico in a chokehold?"

Loco gave the sweetest smile she could muster with her dark plum lips and answered with just as much sugar, "He called me a 'pendeja' after I wouldn't let him grab my waist."

Savalez pinched the bridge of his broad honey brown nose and shook his head. ChicoMadness always wound up in situations like these. Great with music, bad with women. The exec waved off the issue, "I'll talk to him later." He looked up and spoke to everyone in the room, "You're all here because Dowry's got another tour coming up in three months, a club tour. Lumination Rising is going to open for them. It will just be the two of you. We probably will get local openers in different cities to start the show but Ketchup says it's pretty much you two. Lumination, get your record to me done and done by the end of this month. Dowry, you will be sharing practice space at Mindware warehouse."

The women cheered quietly among themselves. Mindware was always seen as Lumination Rising's turf. The Dowry Effect's space was considerably smaller, located in the basement of Delirium. And scary. Dowry nicknamed the studio "The Death Trap" and Lux was always summoned to kill spiders and centipedes. Deborah never wasted a chance to ask for an upgrade from Savalez. This was the first time he let it happen.

Lumination had a different response.

Amos tapped Mars' knee. It was a signal the band developed to help establish better boundaries. Last minute idea from Isaiah after he got flustered with Mars arguing with him over his thoughts.

Mars, what if they find out about you? Amos pondered.

Mars spoke up, "I think I speak for everyone here in Lumination – do they have to use Mindware?" The other guys nodded in agreement.

Nakia pursed her black painted lips and folded her rose brown arms. "Our space is *small*," she said. "And it's *our* tour."

Savalez intervened, "Mars, the space is big enough for the both of you. They can practice as you guys clean up and record. Any other questions?" Everyone knew Savalez didn't want more questions, that was his way to end any conversation.

The room was quiet.

"Bueno. Now, get to work." Savalez got up and left.

Touring practice started immediately. It was already a couple weeks' practice into the tour rehearsals. It was going to be The Sugar and Spikes Tour, starring The Dowry Effect and Lumination Rising as a double headliner show. Fans were abuzz online and heavy promotion was underway. So far, so good.

Mars was in better spirits. He had been home for a little over a month and a half now. Danielle was ecstatic and the girls were beyond excited the day he came home. Amos was just glad to get Mars out of his house. He spent days begging the plumber and electrician to come back. Amos tried to find others but those two had the best rates. Since being home, Mars' dark moods subsided. His skin jagged less, too. He was almost whole again. Isaiah was glad, Dao was cautiously optimistic.

The men of Lumination cleaned up the studio for The Dowry Effect. Any holes they couldn't patch, Amos drafted alibis about that ranged from "y'know, second-hand is still good" to "tour scars, roadies can be careless" to anything else he hoped they would believe. The Dowry Effect brought in their own payload of instruments, gear and mics. They thought nothing of the holes, it was better than their dungeon of a studio that teemed with critters, dust, a flickering light and skeevy producers. Deborah mentioned this as well to Savalez, that he needed to be better to his girl bands. Savalez would never reply. To keep things peaceful (and Mars' secret hidden), both bands penciled in their choice times. The Dowry Effect preferred late afternoons, Lumination Rising liked late mornings.

All was going well until the third week.

Mars was reclined on the faded peach couch with Isaiah, watching a video on the guitarist's phone. It was a video of an iguana trying to eat a cherry tomato, Isaiah couldn't help but to show it to everyone he could. Lux was a few paces away, tuning her clear guitar and testing her effect pedals on her micro-amp, which was covered in silver scribbles, band stickers and cartoon hearts. Her bubblegum peach Bantu knots were covered in small, gold wire cages. Amos and Loco sat in the kitchen area, chatting away in Spanish over Earl Grey. Loco's long triplet of French braids were covered with a black bandana. Dao, Nakia and Deborah were running late, stuck in traffic during a "quick" food run.

Out of the blue, Mars began coughing. His body had fits from time to time but they were never much and never long. Mars would cough out a shard and either Amos would rush over to throw it away or Mars would try to re-absorb the shard through his hand. He fought to not do worse. He was finally back home, Mars wanted nothing more than to stay home.

Isaiah patted Mars on the back lightly. He felt for jags as he patted, nothing stood out. "You ok, Mars?"

All eyes were on Mars as he could feel a couple shards come up. He pulled them both, flat and shank, from his pressed lips. The moment Isaiah spotted the shards, he ducked down in front of Mars to obscure the view. Amos raced over to retrieve the shards. The girls watched, attentive and cautious. When they moved in, Amos warned them that Mars had an odd condition from the explosion but not to worry about it, just let the guys of Lumination Rising care for their own. Any time anyone from Dowry tried to press for more detail, Amos would simply repeat himself: *let Lumination worry about Lumination.*

Amos walked to the trash can with a loosely clasped hand and threw out the shards.

Isaiah tapped Mars on the knee. *Mars, man, you all right?*

Mars nodded as his coughs trailed off. Then the coughing picked back up, another shard was coming. The fits had gotten pretty bad recently. He had been trying to suppress his abilities to avoid discovery for too long. Mars openly hacked and coughed, and three medium shards clattered onto the floor. One shard bounced off the other two and slid to Lux's orange pedal. She looked down at it. Amos spotted Lux's downward stare and traced it to what it was. He would have bowled her over in his dead sprint to pick up the shard but she leapt out of the way in time, clutching her clear guitar. Lux almost landed into her guitar rack, she snagged the corner of an amp for support.

Lux yelled, "What is *with* your cousin, man? Was that ice?"

Loco tipped quickly past the commotion and looked into the trash can. Laid atop a crushed soda bottle were the refused shards. They looked as if bitten from a window pane.

"Lux!" She called out. "It looks like glass! He's got glass in his mouth!" She pulled out her phone, covered in an over-sized gold bell case and a cracked screen. She dashed to her guitarist and Amos, "I'mma call help! He could be blee–"

Amos threw down the shard and grabbed both Loco and her phone. Both he and Isaiah loudly protested the idea.

"No!" yelped Amos as he wrangled the phone away with one hand and held Loco back with the other. Amos struggled, "No! Mars is – ergh – Mars is fine!"

Not keen on how she was handled, Loco jammed into Amos with her shoulder. The impact took Amos by surprise but he regained his footing and held her tighter with one arm. Just as strong as he, Loco began to pry out of the grip. She dug in her gold nails as she screeched, "Lux! Get this fool off me!" Loco stomped on Amos' foot. Her heel met the metal of his steel toe boot.

"Oh, great," she muttered, "you wear the same shoes as me."

Lux threw her guitar over her shoulder, secured with a beaded leather strap, and rushed up to Amos to plant a strong, booted kick square to his back, sending both Amos and Loco to the floor. Loco's phone skittered to the base of the trash can. Loco scurried up faster than Amos and gave him a solid kick to the side, the metal in her boot knocked the wind out of him.

Isaiah still stayed with Mars, crouched and waiting for more glass to come. He heard Amos groan and crumple. Mars was still collecting himself, head hung low as light coughs trailed from him.

Isaiah patted Mars on the knee and rushed out, "Gotta handle this, try to pull yourself together."

With a sharp charge, Isaiah sprang over the couch and tackled both Lux and Loco. His charge was not as solid as he had hoped, and he lost his footing. Amos heard Isaiah's clobbered footwork as he remained on the floor, curled up and clutching his stomach. *That girl kicks like a freight train,* Amos winced.

Though Isaiah stumbled, he managed to get back upright before Lux could kick him in the face. Instead, he caught her thick calf and threw Lux into Loco, downing them both. Isaiah then backed away to pull up Amos and drag him beside the couch. Mars' head was still laid low, he wanted no part of this. This was probably the first fistfight in the studio space.

Loco spotted her phone. She grabbed Lux's wrist and rushed to pick it up. Loco scrolled through her contacts as fast as she could but her phone was slower than her thumb.

Lux yelled out, "What is *wrong* with you?" Her deep brown cheeks were red with fire as she staggered to her feet.

Amos spotted Loco on her phone. As he struggled against Isaiah to get up, he shouted, "Don't call anyone!" No matter how hard Amos tried, his body was still winded. It was a very well-placed kick.

"Mars is fine!" Isaiah yelled. He dropped Amos and ran up to Loco, gunning for her phone.

Lux tackled his side hard, "Stay! *Down!*" They spilled onto the floor. Lux zipped back onto her feet first. She kept steady eyes on Isaiah splayed out on his back.

Fear gripped Amos. He looked at Mars, his head was still down.

"Mars!" Amos begged. "*Please* do something! They'll tell everyone!"

Quiet and calm, Mars got up and turned towards Loco. With Savalez's number gleaming on her screen, it turned into a small field of clear stalagmites. Loco dropped her phone with a quick yelp.

Lux turned her head at Loco's yelp and saw the changed phone. Isaiah looked at the phone from where he laid. The light from the screen illuminated the crystal mountain in a bluish white.

"Everyone will play nice," Mars directed dully. "Everyone."

"How can you do that?" Lux asked.

Mars answered plainly, "The explosion from about a year ago. I can heal faster, mess with glass ... and read minds a little." He had a small smirk.

Loco covered her forehead with her tattooed hands, as if a proper shield.

Tired and a bit annoyed, Mars continued, "I can mainly hear thoughts about *me*. And I'm not breaking into heads *that* much. I've passed fans on the street, I really rather not know what others are thinking, especially about *me*."

Loco lowered her hands slowly.

"This band has been trying to cover for me since. Especially my cuz, Amos. Savalez don't know, no one at the label knows. Just my band, my wife and my kids." The vocalist shrugged, weary of all the commotion, "I guess you both know, too. You can tell Nakia and Deb but don't breathe a word to *anyone* else. Agreed?"

Lux and Loco exchanged glances and looked back at Mars.

Lux nodded at the offer, "Loco and I will agree to that. But! In exchange, none of us gets hurt. One nick on Dowry and we're yellin' to the world, good?"

Mars shrugged, "If you can get that far, sure–"

"You have our word," Amos interrupted. "No harm will come to any of you. Mars' come a *long* way from the day he was in that explosion." He looked at his cousin's flat face, "A *long*, long way."

Loco still stared at the marvel that was her phone. It slowly slid back into a flat screen. Even the cracks on her phone were healed.

Ten minutes later, the rest of the bandmates sauntered in, bulbous bags of lukewarm fast food and energy drinks in tow. They found Mars seated cross-legged on a jagged, ornate table of glass with horned corners in the middle of the practice area. His back was towards them. The studio was completely empty.

Mars droned, "Everyone found out and I got tired."

Dao's stomach dropped. So did the bags of food. Seeing none of the other members, he grabbed Deborah and Nakia's wrists and yanked them towards the door ...

But it was frosted over with jagged shards. The trio screamed. Dao pulled the women away from the door and behind one of the amp towers, away from any possible projectiles the door could lance them with. But they were still in full view of Mars.

Dao demanded, "Stop, man! Where is everyone else?"

"In the warehouse getting clothes for the tour." Mars slid off the table of glass, it disappeared from underneath him. As he sauntered towards the frightened trio, Mars smoothed back his dreads into a thick ponytail. Holding his hair, a cuff of glass appeared from underneath his hands, banding it together.

Dao pulled Deborah and Nakia behind him. He turned his head to the covered side and waited for the worst. He knew Mars would snap again. And here he was, with even more possible victims to create. *Please don't hurt them*, Dao thought. *Just take it out on me and be done but spare them.*

Mars laughed. He clapped a hand on Dao's left shoulder and kneaded it. "I'm changed, remember? You've got nothing to fear." Mars saw the dropped bags and investigated them. "Whatcha get? Burgers and tacos?"

Dao grew angry. He started towards Mars but Deborah and Nakia held him back.

"Let him do what he *wants*," Deborah hissed into Dao's ear.

"Dao, what's going on?" Nakia whispered, tucked between the amp and the sea-gray wall.

"Mars going overboard again," Dao responded through clenched teeth. "Let me handle this." He pulled from the tight grasp of the two women. Neither wanted him to step forward and neither did he. But something had to be done.

Mars fished for the warmest burger in the bags, but he became unsatisfied with his finds.

Storming up to Mars, Dao questioned, "Have you gone back to evil or did Amos let up his leash too much again?"

Finding a single burger he guessed he would like, Mars unwrapped it and took a bite. It had ketchup and no mayo but Mars ignored the disdainful taste. "Nah," Mars answered with a half full mouth. "I just got tired holding it in. Was starting to make me sick." Seeing Dao's angered expression, Mars cleared the glass from the door. "Hey, look, I didn't want those two running off, it was the best I had at the moment. Lux and Loco already found out today." He looked past Dao to the two women pressed against the wall. "Go call them if you don't believe me." Mars finished eating his burger.

A heavy, metal door clanged shut on the other end of the studio. The remainder of the two bands returned from the warehouse, their arms full with bundles of clothing and tally sheets stuffed into their hands to give to Mindware and Delirium later for number crunching.

The moment Deborah spotted Lux and Loco walking between Amos and Isaiah, she sprinted to them, Nakia not far behind.

As Deborah vaulted over chairs and amps, she declared, "Tribe! Rally up!" She skidded to a halt at her bandmates and grabbed their arms, "We are leavin' *now*. Mars is *trippin'*."

Loco and Lux pulled away. They tried to clamor that they were fine but it all fell on deaf ears.

"Deb, Debbie!" Lux attempted to calm Deborah but the vocalist kept pulling at her arm.

Loco reached better ground with Nakia. "Kia, we're *fine*," she asserted. "Mars ain't gonna hurt any of us. He swore!"

Nakia shook her head, her purple braids shimmied with vigor, "Girl, you don't understand what I *saw*."

"He fixed my phone screen! Look!" Loco presented her phone, screen brand new. It wasn't much proof but it was perhaps something.

Sure enough, the cracks were gone but Nakia wondered, *How does this mean Mars ain't gonna hurt us?*

"Because I'm not, Nakia," Mars answered from halfway across the room. "I promised those two I wouldn't. Right, Amos?"

Loco covered Nakia's head and laid it on her shoulder. She chided Mars, "Oooooh, don't be readin' her mind like that!" She mentioned to her confused bassist, "He can read your mind if you think about him."

Nakia scrunched her face in disgust.

Deborah had enough. Amos tried to speak but Deborah cut him off early.

"Boy, I 'on't wanna hear *nothin'* right now," Deborah resisted. She called out to Mars, tapping her thick curl-covered temple, "Ey, Mars! Psychogram just for you, papi!"

Mars stood aghast at the mental verbal carving he received. He was also grateful he couldn't see mental pictures.

"Jeez!" Mars lamented, "Even my uncle from *war* never talked like that. In English *or* in Spanish!"

Deborah nodded with satisfaction. "Eh-henh, that's what I thought!" She tugged at Lux's thick arm. "Tribe! We rollin' *out!* C'mon!"

Amos ran ahead of her, throwing his clothing bundle down in a nearby chair. "Whoa, whoa! Not so fast! None of you can tell Savalez or *any*one else."

Deborah stopped short. "Wait, Savalez don't *know?* How he don't know? He knows *everything.*"

"Not if you spin a good enough tale he'll eat," Amos replied.

"It hasn't been an easy ride for us, either," Isaiah admitted as he placed down his stack of clothes. He joined Amos' side. "We've been workin' hard to keep Mars' abilities under wraps." Isaiah looked at Mars. "And keeping his head as level as possible about it."

Dao added coldly, "Even though sometimes his level is *way* tilted, even with steering."

Mars looked at him. Dao looked back through his

dreads. *You're my brother but I'm never going to forget what you did to me, Mars,* Dao thought.

Mars looked back at the rest of the group. He never imagined life being like this. Either nothing made sense or just seemed too surreal. And there he stood in the middle, trying to survive it all.

Done with it all, Mars scratched his temple and summed up to the The Dowry Effect, "You all can do what*ever* you want but none of you can talk about this to anyone else. Kick us off tour if you want but don't say nothin' to *no* one about what I can do or what you saw. Up to you."

Nakia looked at her bandmates. "Tribe!" She called out. "We vote: Keep Lumination in or nah."

The women exchanged looks. Before deciding, Lux asked Mars, "You promise you ain't gonna be breakin' into anyone's heads?"

Mars scoffed, "Heeeeeell no. Debbie's proof positive of why I usually *don't* if I can avoid it."

Deborah smirked confidently.

Nakia asked, "And you can't make people do stuff?"

"Nah, or else Savalez would probably make me his assistant if he found out," Mars joked.

A light laughter broke out among the two groups.

Lux presented her fist. It was laden with delicate gold stacked rings and a crude smiley face on her middle finger. "I'm in."

Loco stacked her fist on top of Lux's. It was a bit more slender but built with sheer muscle. "I say 'yes'."

Nakia looked at the men of Lumination Rising. *They're not that bad,* she thought. *They've been far better than the Psychonauts.* She remembered bandaging Deborah's hand after Deborah punched the Psychonauts' horn player because he got too handsy during practice. Lumination Rising had a far better reputation, one of the best in the circuit and especially at Delirium.

She stacked her wide fist atop the growing pile. "Lumination can't be that bad," Nakia reasoned with her vote.

All that remained was Deborah. She looked at the yes votes. Biting her gold lip in thought, she ruminated deeply. At worst, Mars could go off the rails. Looking at the men, she thought about what they said about trying to keep Mars on the straight and narrow over his abilities. He was a wild child but not in a bad way, the worst she had ever heard about him was when he punched a cop who was dragging a young girl at a Chicano Pride festival. How he managed to evade capture and charges still eluded her. No rape accusations, decent family-man reputation and lived a fairly clean life. Lumination Rising never got mixed up with any drugs, crime or major hard living. Deborah definitely knew her band had been paired with far worse. She could live with glass being Lumination's biggest secret. There's far worse in the music industry and Deborah had seen her fair share, firsthand.

Deborah topped the stack with her own heavily tatted fist, a bullet on her first and second finger standing out. "Lumination's in!" she declared officially.

Her bandmates cheered at the successful vote, and hugged Deborah. The Punk vocalist turned to the men and announced, "Y'all in!" The men of Lumination beamed brightly. Isaiah clapped a congratulatory hand on Amos' broad shoulder. Deborah continued, "We'll keep y'all itty-bitty secret but let us be clear: you touch my girls, I touch your face! That's rule number one on any Dowry tour. Welcome aboard, compadres!"

Part Two: The Tour

The Sugar and Spikes Tour was underway. At least the prepping part. Two tour buses sat outside Delirium, taking up a sizable amount of curb. One was silver with a curved nose, for Lumination Rising. The other was gold-detailed, brown and flat faced, slated for The Dowry Effect. They both were parked there before the crack of dawn, now the sun hung in the clear morning sky. The day was warm but a little hotter than desired for a spring day.

Both bands were loading up their respective buses; this would be home for the next three months. The tour was slated to be from March to June, ending just before the Fourth of July. The first leg of the tour would be to Texas, then a small break. The men of Lumination looked very forward to that small break, particularly Amos.

In the days and weeks that led up to that morning. Amos kept in close contact with The Dowry Effect about Mars. Mainly on the subject of how to handle him and all the warning signs of when they couldn't. The one thing they agreed on was that the label and fans simply couldn't find out. Lumination had just turned in their album not too long ago and it was already picking up steam, even though the release date was still getting hammered away in-house. Dowry had a couple new unnamed songs for their next album, they presented them to Savalez when he visited tour rehearsal at Mindware. The men of Lumination were astounded by how steadfast and constant the women worked.

Dao stomped up the metal, narrow steps of the tour bus as he hefted on a huge maroon suitcase, the edges of the stairs were worn and scuffed from all the years of use. It was a bit difficult for him to navigate himself and angle his suitcase properly through the narrow passageway of the short stairwell as well as the hard turn into the living area at the front of the tour bus, but he tried. With only one eye fully functional and the other heavily blurred, Dao struggled with anything on his right. The deep scars were better healed but no matter how many salves and lotions he smeared on them daily, they were still there.

Winded from moving the umpteenth thing onto the bus with frustrating half-vision, Dao sat down on the dark, over-softened couch. He sat his luggage on his lap and looked about. The bus was mostly aglow with natural light from the large windows and the lake-shaped mirrors on the ceiling helped expand the luminescence. He sat on the long couch on the left side of the crowded living room. On the right was a small kitchenette, an equally small dining area and a short couch with a flat TV fastened to the wall. The short couch and dining area were already covered with tossed luggage, Dao's was soon to be another addition.

Before Dao could grip his luggage properly to toss on the pile, Isaiah dragged himself and a sizable storage tub aboard. The guitarist grunted and even slipped a bit on the stairs as he struggled with the clear container aboard filled almost to the brim. His arms strained as his black tank top showed light curves of dust from where he fell on the metal steps.

"What on *earth* are you bringing aboard?" Dao asked. He craned his neck and turned his head to look out of his better eye; the tour bus' doorway was on his right.

Straining some, Isaiah answered, "Temple bells for you to pray to, Dali Lama. I am *not* starving on this tour."

"So you draggin' on your whole *fridge?*" Dao questioned.

Isaiah finally got the tub around the narrow corner and into the aisle. It clopped onto the laminate floor after it popped from around the corner, the lid slightly ajar. Revealed inside were snack bars, meal shakes and several bags of trail mix.

Astonished by the amount, Dao said, "We're not going overseas this time. You expect to eat *all* of that?"

Isaiah sat on the floor beside the bin and looked up to Dao, "Nah, I expect to get maybe two bars and Amos sneaking into the rest of my pile. Whatever Amos don't get, Ketchup an' everyone else – you included – gonna devour."

Dao laughed, "I only go into your stash once in a while. Ketchup and Amos are the real squirrels here. You need to stop getting tasty stuff."

"No," Isaiah retorted, half firmly, half-jokingly. "All of you need to start bringing on your own snacks!"

"We do, you just bring way more," Dao smiled. His dreads covered half his face but his grin was full and toothy.

Isaiah got up, dusted himself off and continued dragging the tub into the bunk section. He pressed the small, square button sitting above the bare kitchenette to open the wooden doorway to the bunks. The door slid aside cleanly and revealed a darkened thorax of layered bunks. Three bunks in a stack, two stacks of bunks side by side on both walls. All the claimed ones already had drawn curtains. There were still a few open spaces left.

"Middle bunk's mine!" Isaiah declared as he hefted his tub onto the narrow sleeping space. With a thin mattress, a tiny television hitched in the corner and a half-way decent electrical socket, the bunk wasn't much but it was better than the old RV the band used to tour around in when they first started.

"Okay," Dao replied. "I want a top bunk!"

"I think Mars and Amos claimed those!" Isaiah called back. The two top bunks already had curtains drawn.

"Ahhhh," Dao pondered. "I will take the very bottom bunk, then."

Isaiah spotted several unclaimed bottom bunks. "You got something for Zip-Zips?"

Dao chuckled lightly, "Maaaaaan, stop tryin' to rename my hamster. My brother's lookin' after him."

Isaiah drew the curtains of his and Dao's bunk shut. He went back into the living area and sat next to the bassist.

Slouched and comfy, Isaiah commented, "'Zip-Zips' is a good name for your hamster."

"No, it's not," Dao replied. "He's been 'Chunks' for a long while."

"Your hamster's *fast,* not fat." Isaiah retorted. "We wouldn't have caught him if he didn't get dizzy on Mt. Seung's turntable set when we toured with Stacker St."

"He wouldn't have darted about if you held him right and didn't let him squirm out your hand. I asked if you had him and you said 'yup' and then I look again – off goes Chunks runnin' around, explorin' the big, scary world," Dao rebutted.

"Zips bit me!" Isaiah defended. He still thought he should be rewarded for not punting the mischievous rodent out of shock and pain. Definitely made him reconsider his position on animal rights for a moment.

"Chunks bites everyone. Especially people who eat nut bars. Like you," Dao expressed matter-of-factly. He still hadn't forgotten the near heart attack that clanged in his chest when he saw his small, squishy pet smack to the floor and scurry out of the dressing room into the backstage hallway. How Chunks did not get stepped on or flattened still baffled Dao. However, he was overjoyed when Chunks returned to him in a baseball cap snatched from a random roadie's head. Ketchup was pretty irritated that he had to catch a hamster while managing a tour – a hamster that peed on a turntable set in fear, at that. And bit him, twice.

Amos walked aboard with a tower of folded towels.

Overhearing the conversation, he asked incredulously, "Are you both still arguing over that hamster?"

Dao said, "He is, I'm not." He chuckled, "Isaiah is obsessed with my hamster, still."

In the stairwell of the tour bus behind Amos, Mars remarked, "Dao, did you bring your pet on tour again?"

Dao's humor chilled. "Nah, nah," said Dao as he got up and stretched. "I'm gonna go get my charger and set up the back." He left into the bunk area, where he minded the suitcase he lugged behind him.

Amos and Isaiah exchanged unsteady looks. Dao still had a residual fear of Mars. While Mars had improved in the time leading up to the tour, Dao was never fully convinced. His scars were too heavy a reminder.

Amos moved further into the bus to make space for Mars to come in. Mars' dreads were banded together in a tight braid. He wore a loose, glass bracelet he certainly didn't have on an hour ago. Now that he was back home, Mars had improved by leaps and bounds and he relaxed way more about his abilities. Amos wanted to believe Mars was completely better but he still had his concerns, especially when Mars fell back into his melancholic moods. Danielle always oozed to Amos how well Mars was coping at home so Amos figured Mars mainly slipped back around the band when they were alone.

Mars looked around, "Ah, our new home."

Amos tried to remain upbeat. "Mars, you think you're up for this?"

Mars looked at his cousin and shot a plastic smile, "Why wouldn't I be? Chill, cuz," Mars patted Amos on the shoulder, "I won't frost the crowd."

Dao and Isaiah froze. Amos tried to keep up his bright façade and lightly tapped Mars' hand on his shoulder.

Mars, Amos thought, *knock off the creepy act.* Aloud, the drummer said, "Be chill, okay?"

Mars nodded. He slid off his hand and sat on the couch next to Isaiah. Before he could get comfortable next to the rigid guitarist, a tall, slim man with aged, blotted tattoos all over his reddish-brown skin climbed aboard. It was Ketchup, Savalez's right-hand man, especially for tours. He was checking his tablet as he climbed aboard and looked up to find all of Lumination Rising together ... and not packing.

Ketchup rubbed his thin neck in beleaguered agitation. "'Ey, come on, everyone!" He complained with a heavy accent, thicker than Savalez's. "We got a show tonight! Let's go, let's go, let's *go!*" He scrolled and tapped through the many pages on his tablet. He continued, "Between you guys and the girls, we are *never* going to leave! Savalez want this curb clear in *two hours.* He's getting *sick* of seeing these buses."

The men of Lumination knew what that meant: Sitting buses meant wasted time, wasted time meant wasted money. Wasted money meant angry Savalez.

All of them tinkered out apologies and started dissecting the pile of luggage that sat on the short couch.

As the men put away everything they could on the bus, Ketchup announced, "Okay, muchachos, here are the details: First show is tonight across town at Justa Jamma. It will be just Lumination and Dowry, no guest openers. Doors are gonna open at eight, both of you are having an hour and a half set each. Show starts at nine. Meeker's doin' drums, Jeremy is the guitar tech, Bobo is assistant. All of them are already there, helping with set up for you guys. Dowry's got Kendra on drums, Lakeia doin' guitars and Cutie as their assistant, they're also down there. Mooch is down there, too. He's runnin' the merch table. I'm goin' to get your show sheet for today, we eat at three o' clock." Ketchup walked off the bus.

Hearing Ketchup's voice fade further and further away as he directed others, most of the band sighed. Mars shrugged and kept putting his things away. His bunk was at top and on the opposite of Dao's side (to the alleviation of the bassist). After Mars emptied all he wanted in his bunk – his tablet, his pillows, his blanket and headphones – Mars made a plate of glass over the opening of his bunk and drew the curtain tight. Amos saw but he said nothing.

Mars reopened his bunk for a moment to reach through the glass and pull out his navy-blue suitcase. He drew the curtain tight again and walked past everyone to get off the tour bus. He walked his suitcase to the open luggage compartment. It was cumbersome but manageable to carry.

As he shoved his luggage in, Mars heard Deborah call his name. Looking up, Mars saw Deborah jogging up to him. She had on rounded sunglasses, unlaced boots and a ripped-up shirt layered over a plain tank top and dark military cargo pants.

"Hey, Mars," greeted Deborah. She lurched towards him to give a hug but resisted at the last moment.

"I'm not a cactus, Deb," Mars said.

Unsure of herself and Mars, Deborah chuckled and remarked, "That's good. How are you doing today?"

Mars answered, "The same as always." He waved and walked away without another word, back onto the bus.

Deborah wanted to feel tossed off at his abrupt departure but Amos warned her not to. She remembered him explaining, *Mars has his moody moments, try not to get pissed off about it. It's practically bait but don't take it.* So, Deborah tried to shrug it off and returned to her bus.

The gold bus bustled with activity. Every member of Dowry was well underway with unpacking and loading. Everyone had already called their bunks and now they were making the bus homey. The Dowry Effect was always on the road so they usually loaded the quickest.

Their bus interior looked very similar to Lumination's, only the color of the wood paneling was a bit different and there were gray details lined throughout the bus. Lux was setting up the electric kettle and boxes of tea bags in the kitchenette area behind the dining area. She had already set up the coffee maker, an electric kettle and a stackable food steamer. Loco was in the back room of the tour bus, plugging up power strips and chargers. Dowry members always treated the back room as "The Everything Room", it was the place for meetings, primping, recording and decompressing. Nakia sat on the long couch, typing away on Dowry's various social media sites with her decorated laptop. The lid was encrusted with small guitars and crystals in a detailed argyle pattern.

"Tribe! Can everyone go into the back? Quick, quick meeting," Deborah announced.

Everyone looked up. Loco called out, "I'm already here! And wi-fi is a go, Debbie!"

The remaining members piled into the back. It was a small room crowded with a curved couch and a minuscule dining area that could barely seat two or three. There was an embedded television and audio decks overhead, all off, and another lake-shaped mirror on the ceiling. Deborah closed the door between the bunks and the back room.

"What's going on, Deb?" Lux asked.

"Mars," Deborah reported. "He may be startin' up soon. I'mma tell Amos–"

"Wait, wait!" Loco interjected. She covered her forehead, "Can Mars hear us now?"

Deborah replied, "Amos said he doesn't have too huge a range and tries to ignor–"

"'Ignore' don't mean 'can't hear'," Nakia noted.

"We're *fine*," Deborah assured. She continued, "Amos is gonna get a heads up. Y'all be careful around him. Ketchup don't know nothin', Savalez don't know nothin', remember that."

"Ain't Ketchup gonna stay on their bus?" Lux asked.

Deborah shrugged. "That's all on them. As for us, keep an eye on Mars. He's really changed since the accident. He used to be … sunnier. Now he's like a threatin' storm. Amos really wasn't jokin' about that."

At the front of the bus, Dowry heard, "Ladies! Can I see everybody up front or should I come back later?"

Quietly, Deborah reminded her band, "Be careful, stay safe, say nothing." Loudly, she said, "'Ey, Ketchup, we were just wrappin' up! Give us a minute, okay?"

"Okay!" Ketchup responded.

Deborah asked everyone, "Is everyone cool?"

Her fellow band members nodded.

The lead vocalist took a breath for herself. "Okay, then. Let's go." She turned around and opened the sliding door.

Ketchup waited at the front, busy with his tablet. His dark red shirt fitted him loosely and he had his tour passes and lanyards already clipped to his black pants. The laminated passes had a silver holographic outline on the border. The name of the tour glittered with a pink to dark fuchsia fade in bold letters. He held his tablet by his side like a clipboard, its screen beamed bright with numbers, places and times. Behind the tablet was a sheet of paper.

"Ladies!" Ketchup cheered. "Looks like you're almost ready to go! Lumination is about done and I got your show sheet right here. Today is Justa Jamma, all the info I told all of you earlier today is on this sheet." Ketchup pulled the sheet out from behind his tablet and dug in his pocket for neon yellow tape. He ripped off two pieces and affixed the sign to the narrow wall behind the driver's seat. It had all their set times, where they were, what time zone they were in, where they were going next and when they had to leave.

Ketchup cleared his throat, and announced, "Everyone else is already at the venue. After the show, Cutie, Lakeia and Kendra are gonna be on this bus. The boys are on the other bus. I'm going to go, you all finish getting ready." He left the bus as the band waved him goodbye. Ketchup left the door open.

Nakia muttered among her bandmates, "I feel *so* bad for them. Lumination better have their act *tight* and together."

Her bandmates agreed.

In two hours flat, both buses were on the road. The first venue was not far away, only a forty-five minute drive and they were already half-way there.

On Lumination's tour bus, Dao and Isaiah chatted with Ketchup at the front of the bus over light topics, Amos and Mars were in the back with the door closed.

Reclined across the curved couch with his shoes off, Mars looked out the window, bored. Amos was in the middle of another lecture, seated on the other end of the couch.

"...Mars, I'm not tryin' to be a pest. Mars, are you even listening?"

Mars trailed his languid eyes to his cousin. "Every word," he droned. Mars gave a gaping yawn and held his hands together, inches apart. Between them, a glass puzzle cube materialized. He toyed with it as he repeated dully, "Be a good boy. I'm somehow not a monster. Don't frost fans. Hide what I really am from Ketchup, Mooch and practically everyone else." A thought struck Mars. He spun the cube single-handedly into the air casually, where it disappeared into nothing, "Wait … exactly how long is my leash this tour?"

Amos stared at Mars deadpan. Mars re-materialized the puzzle cube as Amos tried to explain, "Mars, I'm tryin' to keep you safe. Danielle would have a heart attack if your …"

"Affliction," Mars offered.

"*Ability* wound up on a gossip site or something," warned Amos. He never cared for celeb magazines or sites but now he had countless alerts for them on his phone, under "glass, Lumination Rising, Mars, attack".

Mars rolled his eyes with a dark smirk. "You … The offer still stands." The puzzle cube floated between Mars' hands as it sharpened itself into a long spike. Mars grasped it and held it to Amos.

Amos looked at the spike. *Mars, why again?* He lamented in his mind. Aloud, he said, "Put it away."

The spike disappeared. Mars pulled his hand away and laid it in his lap.

"Just be the old Mars in front of our fans, okay?" Amos asked.

Mars nodded, "Sure."

"Also," Amos added, "I'm not gonna make you wear hats or whatever but please try not to frost out on stage."

Mars sighed, "Sure."

In Mars' khaki pocket, his phone rang. It was a simple kalimba tune: Danielle.

Amos got up, steadying himself with the sway of the

moving bus. "Tell Dani I said 'hi'," he said. Amos opened the door and left, closing the door behind him.

Mars fished out his phone and answered it with a caring tone, "Hey, honey."

"Hey, Mars, how are things? Everything off to a good start?" Danielle was in her car, Mars could hear the traffic outside. She was asleep when he left, it was so early in the morning. At least he left no shards behind, he checked.

"Everything is fine so far," Mars assured. "How was dropping off the girls? Did Violet forget her pencil case again? She seems to be losing it a lot this past week."

"Everything went smoothly, honey. The girls are fine. They wish they could have seen you go, though. Vivvi was a little sad this morning," said Danielle. She was glad Mars sounded bright.

Mars frowned a little, "Awww, I'll video call her when I can after or before the show."

"She would like that," Danielle smiled. "Are you sure you're okay, Mars? Will the tour be too hard for you? There's so many people." She remembered seeing Mars come home from tour practice, worn and concerned. The tour worried him endlessly. Nary a single night passed where he didn't tell her how much he grew terrified of the stage and crowds. He improved over time but she knew better, she knew Mars. Also, Amos also gave her regular updates. She just wanted Mars to be okay.

Mars gazed out the window at all the passing cars. He answered honestly, "I … I don't know, honey. I'm a little scared. I hope it'll be alright and nothin' happens."

"You think it would be okay for me and the girls to be at the show tonight?" Danielle asked, hesitant. Any other time would have been a no-brainer but not now. Too many things have changed.

Mars thought on it for a moment. He loved seeing his family at his shows but he didn't want his daughters to see a horrible accident should one occur.

"Bring them," he decided. Mars hoped seeing his girls would lower his likelihood of an accident happening.

"You sure?"

Mars' voice perked at the thought, "Yeah, I'm sure. Make sure they finish their homework first. I think Vivvi rushes through hers or says she's done when she's not."

Danielle agreed, "Yeah, her Language Arts teacher told me that today when I was dropping them off, I ran into her."

"Figured as much," Mars sighed. He wasn't exactly a sterling student himself growing up, he used to do the same, on top of cutting up whenever he could. At least Vivica wasn't causing trouble, just rushing or skipping work. Violet was a bit more boisterous. Dao used to joke that he couldn't tell which parent she got it from.

"I'll tell her if she finishes her homework on time, we can see Daddy play. That should give her incentive," Danielle said.

Mars snickered, "I hope so. I'll put everyone on the list. We go on at nine and have an hour and a half set." Out of restlessness, Mars produced a glass coin and flipped it back and forth across his knuckles.

"Okay, see you there," said Danielle. "Love you, honey."

"Love you, too," Mars said.

Danielle hung up.

Mars pocketed the phone and sighed. Talking to her made life worth living but he still wondered if things would be better for them without him. Back home, things were better than before he left, but not by much on some days. At least he would check if the house was empty before attempting to swallow shards. He did notice all the house cleaners were now in powder form the week he came back. Only after the first try did Mars learn it was like swallowing bitter sand. Hardly any went down his throat and he had to spit the rest out. He never tried again.

By himself and in an enclosed room, Mars tried to savor the moment. It was tour time, these moments would be few and fleeting. Mars looked at the small table on the other end of the curved couch. With little focus, glimmering, icy stalagmites rose from the tabletop. Mars then gandered at the mirrored ceiling, down slid thick stalactites with many jagged sharp points. They almost reached the crown of his head. His skin still surged but the more he used his abilities and kept a level head, the less it happened. Same with his shards, he found random ones less and less. Within the last week, he only found one in his shoe when he came home. He would have swallowed it but Violet came in to show him a kitten video. Instead, Mars tossed the shard before she could see.

His dreads unbraided itself, each tendril gleamed with a light cover of glass. One dread presented itself before him.

The end of the dread drew into a sharp, crystallized point. Each of the dreads did.

There was a knock on the door.

A couple dreads rose lazily with daggered points as Mars asked, "Who is it?"

"Isaiah, holmes. Can I come in?"

Mars smirked and raised the stalactites above Isaiah's height. "Come in."

The guitarist opened the door. Shocked by what laid before him, he nearly stumbled out of the room. Isaiah hurried to shut the door behind him and hissed at Mars, "Man, you're–"

"'–Gonna blow your cover.' I know, I know," Mars mocked quietly. The room slowly shifted back to normal, his hair re-braided itself. "If I don't blow off some steam and suppress my 'abilities'–" Mars used air quotes "–they start showing up on their own. Wouldn't that be bad?"

Isaiah was riveted, speechless.

"Do you want to get Amos?" Mars suggested politely.

Isaiah shook his head, stiff as a board. All Mars could hear across his mind was a long line of worried expletives in jumbled English and Spanish.

"Everything fine?" Mars asked. His tone was filled with sarcastic care.

The guitarist stammered out, "We a-are, we're gon-gonna be a-at Jamma soon. I'm-I'mma go now." Isaiah patted the wall for the button blindly. When he heard the door slip open, Isaiah stepped out the room backwards and closed the door with a press of the button on the other side.

Mars smirked to himself. He continued looking outside the window.

Isaiah stumbled to the front of the bus. Both the moving vehicle and what he saw unsteadied his footing. It was a rare sight for Isaiah to see Mars use his abilities so freely. Still scared him nonetheless each and every time.

At the front of the bus sat the rest of the band and Ketchup. They were engrossed in an action movie that played on the television. Isaiah plopped down next to Dao.

Terrified and jittery, Isaiah pulled out his phone, opened the notes app and tapped out a rushed message. He nudged Dao and showed it.

Mar is icin out in teh bac
tel Amso

Dao looked up and saw Isaiah's fretful face. Isaiah mouthed, "Glass. Ev-vry-*where*."

The bassist's face fell. *We're all probably goin' to die before this tour even starts*, he worried.

The door to the back room slid open with a light tap. Mars sauntered out, swaying with the movements of the bus. He drifted to the front of the bus and sat in the empty dining area. Isaiah quickly pocketed his phone.

Eyes fixed on the television, Mars asked, "What are we watching?"

Enraptured by the explosive chase scene on the screen, Ketchup answered, "Amos and Dao found something. I think it's almost done."

"Ah, alright," Mars said. He kicked back and made himself comfortable.

"Hey, Mars?" Isaiah asked. He tried to suppress the shake in his voice. He had never regretted cutting Drama class so much back in school until now. The time he spent at the arcade around the corner was amazing but now he wished for an extra life.

Mars looked at him, "Yeah?" His expression was normal, his tone was plain.

Isaiah checked past Dao and Amos for a moment, Ketchup was still glued to the television. He tapped his temple and said, "Nothin', man."

Mars heard in Isaiah's mind, *Mars, I ain't mean to freak out back there. It just surprised me.*

Mars shrugged at Isaiah and went back to the movie. He willfully ignored anything else Isaiah mentally said next.

A few minutes later, the tour buses docked on an empty sparse city street in front of a venue with big, dark windows. One of the large windows was a digital show marquee. Giant letters scrolled along in a pink to purple fade:

The Dowry Effect and Lumination Rising TONITE!

There were already a handful of fans lined up at the onyx double doors. They stood behind the line of aluminum gates that streamed to the entrance. Everyone watched the tour buses dock in, a few fans bubbled with anxious joy. A different line of gates led to the open doors of the backstage area, a scraped up pair of double doors with a blotchy thick coat of black paint. Roadies milled back and forth through the doors, between the black equipment trailers and Justa Jamma, just like they had all morning.

The bus parked. Ketchup stood up and stretched, his tablet clenched in hand. He announced, "Okay, muchachos. We are *here*. Bunks Manny is the promoter for the show. I'm going to check in with him. You guys chill out here. Soundcheck is probably going to be in a couple hours. Keep your phones *on* – oh, and text me who's gonna be on the guest list, okay?"

The band members nodded.

Ketchup dug out his phone. Glued to the screen, he scrolled through the millions of problems waiting for him. Blindly, he said, "Okay, I'm off. Hit me if you need me and let's have a good show." He exited the bus, followed by the driver, a grandfather of a man with balding white hair and a jutting belly.

The tour bus door clinked shut. Solace at last. The men of Lumination Rising lowered all the accordion paper shades on the bus. Mars pulled out his phone and texted his short list to Ketchup. His head felt a little fuzzy. It was the leanest list he had ever sent, especially for home shows, but lesser was better.

"Amos," Mars said, "Dani and the girls are comin'."

Amos prowled around Isaiah's bunk for a quick snack while the guitarist peeked under the blinds. "Really?" Amos asked. "You think it's okay?" Slip and sly, Amos snuck out three snack bars from Isaiah's bunk. He pocketed two and passed one to Mars when he walked up to his cousin.

"I think so," Mars replied.

Dao reviewed the taped show sheet by the driver station, "The kids are coming?"

Mars nodded, "Yeah, Dani said they really want to be here."

A small, lopsided smile slid onto Dao's face, "I can't wait to see them. Remember when Violet kept calling Amos 'Uncle Amy' for the longest time?" He laughed warmly at the memory.

Everyone tittered and snickered but Amos laughed uneasiest.

Amos waved the memory off, "Yeah, yeah, yeah ... Then you all called me that for *weeks*." Amos passed Dao and gave him a snack bar. Dao reciprocated with a pat on the shoulder.

Mars' head buzzed softly. He couldn't press it down. It was the thoughts of others:

I hope I get to meet Mars!
Mars is here!
Freakin' out! Freakin' out! Mars is on that bus, he has to be!
'Ey, I might meet Mars today! I'mma be at the gate!

The thoughts swept Mars into a sort of dizzy spell. He could hardly hear his own thoughts. Mars staggered to his bunk and grabbed his headphones. They were black, wireless and glass spikes covered the ears. He slid them on, connected to his phone and tried to drown out the noise with some pulsing glitch rock. Most of the thoughts were overtaken by the music but still they pushed against his temples like rushing waves.

Mars dragged himself over and slopped down onto the long couch. He has passed fans on the street but that was one or three, out and about. But this, this was a mounting crowd of fans and ones that *specifically* wanted to see him. This mortified him. The whispers of voices piled into one loud hum of cacophony static filling his brain.

Amos glanced at Mars and looked again. Mars sat there with his headphones and a lost, hopeless stare. Dao noticed as well and tapped Isaiah on the shoulder. The bassist then tugged the guitarist back to gain some distance for the both of them.

The drummer tried to scan Mars' wide and empty eyes. They were still and distant.

"Mars, man, you there?" Amos placed a ginger hand on Mars' forearm. He snatched it back when Mars' skin moved.

Mars could hear nothing but the music and the surging thoughts of others. He got up and started towards the backroom with uneasy footsteps.

Amos hurried behind and clutched Mars' wrist, "Mars! Talk to me, man!"

Mars snatched his wrist away and created a thick, frosted glass wall between him and the rest of the band.

Amos sighed with compressed anger to the rest of the band, "Annnnnnd Mars is starting up again. On the first day of tour. We are *so* screwed."

Isaiah asked, "What do we do? Ketchup sees this and Savalez is gonna trip for *sure*."

Dao guessed, "Better for Mars to freak out now than on stage?"

Amos shot, "Not if he don't get out there in the first place!" He banged on the glass fiercely. "Mars! Come on, holmes!"

The glass spiked, backing away Amos. The spikes receded and smooth, dense writing appeared.

> Go Away.
> Go Away.
> Go Away.

"Progress!" Amos announced, sarcastically.

Determined, Amos went to the small kitchenette and rifled through the top cabinet until he found a box of thick markers. Amos pulled out a marker and ripped off the cap to write on the glass in hasty letters:

> No. Come Out
> - A

The embedded writing in the glass shifted and responded:

> I can hear EVERYONE
> Please take my head off
> Make it stop
> MAKE IT STOP

Amos' eyes widened. He banged on the glass as he yelled, "Let me in! Let me–" Amos interrupted himself to scribble on the glass:

LET ME IN

- A

Dao and Isaiah watched, unmoved from where they stood. They both looked over at the tour bus' stairwell from time to time, watching for Ketchup.

The glass wall opened up, perfectly sized for Amos. The drummer rushed through, the wall resealed behind him. He found Mars in the back room, seated on the floor with his back to the door. Mars was curled up like a child, thick glass grew everywhere. It grew out of Mars' braid in jagged clusters. The world was a silent capsule, only the tinny music that bled out of his headphones marked any noise.

"Help me, Amos," Mars choked. "Just end me already."

"Mars," Amos stated. "You gotta fight this. You gotta get your head straight. There's only a handful of people out there, it's gonna get worse tonight. You gotta focus."

"Just kill me–"

"No! Mars, you are slippin' back and *fast*." Amos walked over to Mars and squatted down in front of his cousin, who was deeply shrunken into himself. The drummer continued, "Mars, look at me and *focus*." Amos clasped Mars' face to stare into his bewildered eyes. "*Focus*. Focus on your breathing like I taught you. Turn down the music and *breathe*."

126

On the other side of the glass wall, Dao and Isaiah heard the tour bus door click open. They both rushed to crowd the stairwell. Opening the door was a shorter, stocky man with a faded mohawk tipped platinum silver. Tattoos covered a burnt gold neck and hands. It was Mooch. He poked himself in halfway for privacy from the prying fans.

"'Ey, guys!" he cheerfully greeted. "Are you guys ready? Soundcheck is about to start soon. Or do you guys wanna eat first?"

Dao and Isaiah exchanged looks. Isaiah spoke first, "We'll eat first but can you give us ten–"

"–Fifteen," Dao interjected.

"–Twenty-five minutes? Emergency band meeting," Isaiah said.

Dao nodded in agreement to Isaiah, he hoped Mooch would buy it.

Mooch eyed the bassist and guitarist, a bit unsure. "Allllllllllright then. Half an hour. Text me when you're all done, okay?"

Dao agreed warmly, "You got it."

Isaiah jabbered on in anxious Spanish, "We'll meet you in a – uh, thanks."

Mooch left and shut the door. Dao and Isaiah exhaled a deep breath.

Isaiah muttered in English as he tugged on one of his curls, "What the *hell* are we going to do?"

Dao grumbled, "I have no clue."

The glass wall fell. Dao and Isaiah heard the dual footsteps of Amos and Mars coming to the front of the tour bus. Amos guided his cousin from behind by the shoulders. The back room was back to normal. Mars walked limply, his headphones around his neck and his eyes plagued with a busy mind.

Isaiah approached Mars with a step or two. He asked, "Mars, are you going to be able to do the show tonight?"

Unsteady, Mars replied, "I – I don't know. It's hard … as it is. I hear way too many thoughts. Too … too many."

Amos chipped in, "Mars is having a hard time but tell Ketchup an' 'nem he's got a headache or gettin' sick or somethin'. Anything, okay?"

Dao felt concerned but he couldn't help but feel annoyed all the same. "More stories, Amos?"

Amos rebutted, "Dao, we can't be havin' Ketchup or Savalez discover Mars! Especially not like this."

Dao argued, "Amos … Man, Mars is our brother but *when*? When will it be the *time*? Dude, he–"

"Mars *needs* us now, we will sort that out *then*–"

"No, *you* will sort it out and tout us a bunch of lines!" Dao blared. "Mars can't be hidden forev–"

"I'm right *here*," Mars interrupted. Though his voice shook, it was still laced with irritated resolve.

"Mars," Dao said firmly, "we *know*. But Amos playin' Spin Doctor forever an' ever is *not* helping us!"

"What?" Amos said.

Isaiah jumped in, "Whoa, whoa, stop. Stop, stop, *stop*. Dao, Amos is playin' 'Spin Doctor' because Mars need our help – but! But!" Dao tried to argue over Isaiah but Isaiah was louder, "Buuuuuut! Amos, Dao has a point! Mars can't be hidden forever and sometimes hiding Mars puts *all* of us in danger – Mars. *Mars.* Please. Pleeeaaaaaase let me finish – Dao took a major hit and we all ran with the tale. Even when there were a million holes in your story, we ran with it. We can't be doing this forever. We are on our first show – haven't even done *soundcheck* yet – and we're havin' a crisis. How the *hell* are we going to survive tour like this? Mars, you could slip on camera–"

Amos interjected to his cousin, "Mars, just focus and–"

"It can happen, *Amos!*" Isaiah crowed. "Ain't *nothin'* but cameras out there and you think Mars won't slip *once*? We got over twenty stops on the whole tour and you think Mars won't frost out on stage?"

"He's right, cuz," Mars agreed.

"You've done well for our rehearsals!" Amos told Mars.

Dao coldly added, "And when he didn't, there was a new story to tell when it was more than Dowry and us in the room. You know Savalez snuck 'no glass bottles or cups' into our rider, right? Even the Psychonauts don't have that and they have regular *fights* at their shows."

Amos was left speechless.

Isaiah said, calmer, "Mars, *please* get your head in the game. We want you around but you have to get it together, man. Amos, you can't cover forever. *We* can't cover forever. Tours are hard enough as it is without mind reading and glass powers. And touring is what we will all be doing for the next three *months*."

Dao shrugged, "I agree with Isaiah. Maybe we *should* let Ketchup in the loop."

"*What? No!*" Amos harshly rejected. "Have you gone coo-coo? He–"

Dao defended, "It sounds like a bad idea because usually tellin' Ketchup is basically tellin' Savalez but maybe–"

"No way!" Amos resisted.

A loud cheer erupted outside.

"Dowry must of gotten off the bus," Mars summed. The pressure in his head died down some.

They heard an excited male fan scream, "Te amo, Loco!"

Loco yelled right back, "Te amo, random fan!"

"My name is Marquis!" the energized fan yelled.

"I love that name! We will see you tonight!" Loco responded bubbly.

The crowd cheered again.

Isaiah rubbed his head in frustration. "Can we get off the bus, please? So we don't starve to death? Mars, what do you need to get off this bus?"

Mars hesitated. The murmuring died down but only because the fans were distracted. He knew that the moment he steps off the bus, the thoughts will crash into him again and stronger. There was no way he could handle that.

"Bag over your head?" Isaiah suggested with acidic politeness.

Mars sighed, "I'm just going to have to get very far away from them until show time. Let's be quick."

"Thank you, God and happy Buddha!" Isaiah crowed.

Isaiah and Dao headed towards the door, Amos steered Mars behind them. Dao pulled the heavy, metal latch and opened the weighted door. Outside waited a hefty crowd of fans. They cheered and screamed as the men of Lumination Rising hurried past them. Mars kept his head down as Amos led him with an arm over his shoulders. The men waved as they walked inside quickly.

They kept walking, guided by venue workers, to the catering room. The further Mars got away from the fans, the better his head felt.

The catering room was a mid-sized room, cavernous with its gray walls and spats of random graffiti. Long tables covered in paper cloth lined the walls, surrounded by tour workers. Each table held several silver trays kept warm with little blue burners underneath. Small circle tables filled the rest of the space. They, too, were covered with white paper cloths. The room buzzed with roadies on break, caterers, tour crew and The Dowry Effect.

Hardly anyone noticed Lumination Rising come in and even less cared. To the roadies and tour crew, they were regular people. Everyone was there to do a job, not be starstruck. Of course, Mars heard a few passing thoughts about him but they were easier to blot out. Though, Mars did get a stream of thoughts from Ketchup about his, Mars, sound levels. The tour manager was entirely certain the sound engineer was either a deaf idiot or a careless buffoon. Mars guessed the sound engineer was consumed with other matters entirely, given the silence of his thoughts.

The band moved through the catering line like weary school children. Dao finished fixing his plate first, a loaded dish filled with salad, hummus and hard boiled eggs, and looked for a place to sit. He spotted Dowry's table.

Dao walked through a small cluster of tables and pulled up a chair. It was difficult to navigate with one good eye, he tried the best he could to not bump into anything but he still clipped the back of a couple chairs.

Close enough to the table to be heard without shouting, Dao asked, "Mind if I sit here?"

Mealtime was well underway at the Dowry's table. Ample food piled everyone's plate and phones were scattered on the table but there was still some space left.

Deborah checked the faces of her bandmates and said, "You're fine. Sit, sit." As Dao sat between empty seats, she asked, "How was your ride?"

Dao picked up what she meant, "A little rocky but nothing too serious. It's the first day of tour, you know how it goes."

Lux nodded as she chewed. After she cleared her mouth, she assured, "Let us know if you need anything."

"Nah, we're fine." Dao watched Mars pick his plate, closely shadowed by Amos, who did the same. "Bull wrangling is what we do best in Lumination." Dao picked up the fork on his plate and started eating his egg-topped salad.

Soon, Isaiah joined the table once he spotted Dao.

"Can I sit here?" Isaiah asked Dowry.

Loco replied warmly, "Sure, sure!"

Isaiah sat down between Dao and Nakia, everyone shifted to make ample room.

"I can't wait for the show tonight!" Isaiah bubbled. He sorted out his clear plasticware and started cutting his sauce-covered steak. The savory smell made his stomach mumble a subtle growl.

Nakia said, "We're closing out the night, you guys are opening it." She sprinkled pepper on her onion slathered steak and french fries.

Isaiah and Dao nodded.

Dao added, "And we're to San Jose next, right?"

Everyone in Dowry nodded.

"I thought," Dao pondered between bites, "I thought we were doing an L.A. show?"

Lux replied blandly, "Management. Savalez said he was told L.A. was too crowded with shows already. He wanted to include smaller markets, anyways."

Isaiah chimed, "Ahhhh, I guess that makes sense."

"We're still doing Alive by Sunrise, right?" Nakia asked. Her plate of creamy shrimp scampi was almost empty.

Loco said, "I think so." She thumbed through the tour itinerary on her phone. She found the Phoenix rock club. "Yup," she confirmed, "Club Alive by Sunrise is next week."

Nakia wondered, "You think B will be there or is he still out?"

Dao chuckled, "Probably still in Bali. He *always* wanted to go." He broke up one of the hardboiled eggs over his salad with his fork. The salad was colorful, filled with immense leafy greens, berries, nuts, croutons and a drizzled sweet balsamic dressing. He was thankful that someone in catering finally read the rider all the way through. Some shows, catering would have practically nothing but water that stuck to his vegetarian diet.

Isaiah snickered as well, "You would have thought it was heaven on earth, man."

Deborah said, "It pretty much is. None of this travelin' circus," she loosely gestured to the buzzing room. "It's quiet and nice but he dipped too quick."

"He wanted a break," Mars said as he approached the table. "I totally get it." He pulled out a chair between Lux and Loco. Amos was not too far behind. He sat next to Mars, beside Loco.

"Ain't Yamato painting the walls at Alive, though?" Lux asked. She scooped together the last of her pasta salad onto her fork and ate it. A lone hamburger stuffed with countless fixings and five sauces remained on her plate.

Deborah inquired, "He is?"

Nakia nodded, "Yeah, Yama is half in-his-feelings, half bein'-artsy and painting up a wall in B's club. It looks good, though."

Loco gushed, "B's gonna love it, you know he would."

Amos checked his plate, filled with smothered chicken cutlets, hamburgers and a clutch of fries. He grasped his plastic fork but looked for something else. "I think I dropped my knife somewhere."

Mars pressed his hand to the table next to Amos' plate. When he removed it, there laid a glass knife. It looked exactly like the clear plastic knives.

"Here you go," Mars offered in a quiet voice.

Everyone fell silent and still.

"Uhhhhh … thanks," Amos said as he took the knife. It

was light, clear and strong. He sliced his food, it cut like the sharpest razor.

"You're welcome," Mars said, a bit flatly. He looked around the table and asked with a low tone, "Hm, why did everyone stop eating? How can you all hide me if you all do things like this?" He coldly joked, "I promise there's no glass in anyone's food. Not even mine."

Amos nudged Mars, "You're fine, dude. Promise." He ate some of his sliced cutlets. Deborah also began eating again, slowly.

Ketchup approached the table, tablet basking and Mooch in tow. Everyone looked up when Ketchup beamed, "So glad the familia is all together. Life made easy." He tapped through his tablet, "Lumination, you guys need to soundcheck now. Dowry, you guys soundcheck later after them. The instruments are mostly set up, everyone's guest lists are in and the merch booth is up. Mooch is gonna work merch but talk to him, Cutie or Bobo if anyone needs anything. They are your assistants and runners. Savalez is probably gonna be at this show – and by 'probably', I mean 'definitely' – so happy faces, everyone. The show is nearly sold out and everything is going to plan. Lumination, get going."

"We just sat down to eat," Dao lamented.

Ketchup vexed, "Dao, holmes, you can come back. Soundcheck is *now*. I'm not tryna hear any nonsense if your bass or mic sounds awful."

The men of Lumination covered their plates with napkins and got up to follow Ketchup and Mooch. The women of Dowry continued to eat and talk among themselves.

As the group of men walked down the backstage hall to the stage, Ketchup passed out Lumination's credentials. Each member received a glittering, all-access pass to clip to their belt loops. Ketchup handed several to Mooch to run back to Dowry.

The front of house was quite standard of any venue with a decent budget. Large pit, not too big a stage, ample sound system. The aluminum gates were already set up before the stage. The sound technician sat in his dark booth behind the pit area, ready for work. He looked beleaguered and chewed out. The lights were low, only the stage was illuminated.

Soundcheck was quite possibly the most normal part of the band's day. Perhaps the only normalcy they will have all day. Mars was like his old self again, kind and peppy. He was happy, light-hearted and even tossed silly jokes as the sound techniuan checked their levels. The guitars and bass sounded fine, the mics were a little watery but that was simply how the sound system of Justa Jamma was.

Dao kept a safe distance from Mars on stage. Mars could hear Dao mentally calculate his every movement. Mars moved two spaces, Dao moved three. Mars couldn't blame him.

After soundcheck was over almost an hour later, Lumination went back to the catering room to pick up their plates. It was emptier now, everyone else was back to work. Venue workers led the band to their dressing room, it was next to Dowry's. Lumination Rising's door was signified with a print-out of their logo, which was a bold L and R with the R balanced atop the space of the L. Beneath it was their band name. On Dowry's door was a logo of Aztec markings as sound waves emitted from the outline of a cowrie shell. Beneath that was their name, typed out as well.

The dressing room was small and a little cramped with couches and a small coffee table covered with snacks and paper cups. The walls were white, and speckled gray tiles graced the recently swept floor. The many tall windows were either frosted or textured for privacy. Wedged in the corner was a narrow door that led to a pint sized bathroom with a half working toilet and a shower stall with no curtain. The bathroom was the size of a closet but at least a shower existed. Some venues had no such amenities at all and there were quite a few of those stops on this tour.

Isaiah plopped down on the pleather couch, careful not to spill his plate of shrimp scampi and breaded fish. He laid his plastic plate on the small table and continued eating. Amos sat beside him and did the same. Amos didn't get big servings like usual, he was too busy tailing Mars without being too obvious. Dao sat on a different couch and ate with the plate balanced on his lap. Mars developed a horned chair and jagged table in the corner of the room, away from the door, and continued eating his steak and cutlets with silverware he materialized himself. Amos shook his head and continued on his fries.

At least Mars is not in front of the door, Amos thought.

There were ten minutes of silence and eating, then there was a rapping at the door.

"It's Bobo! I got Mindware!" he said. He almost sounded like Ketchup, just a few years younger.

Amos called out, "Give us a minute!" He swatted at Mars to get rid of the chair and table.

Mars picked up his plate and complied, annoyed. The chair and table sank back into the floor.

"Come in!" Amos said.

Bobo opened the door, he was a built, cherry-brown skinned man with a bald head. He wore a loose black shirt with olive, worn pants and carried a cardboard box piled with folded shirts.

"Got clothes for all of you to wear on stage, just got pressed yesterday," Bobo said.

Isaiah said, "Thanks, Bobo. How goes it?"

Mars re-braided his dreads using glass behind Bobo's back. Dao and Amos tried to hide their disbelief as they sat before the assistant. Isaiah was more focused on the conversation.

Bobo replied, "Ah, it goes, man. My sis is coming home for the holidays, she just told me."

Isaiah responded with interest, "Oh, that's cool. She's still in school, right?"

"Yup," Bobo affirmed. "Business major. She likes it. Oh, speaking of, you guys have a lean guest list this show. Ketchup wanted to know if that is everyone. Right now, it's just Dani and the girls."

"That's all," Dao said firmly.

Bobo cocked a confused eyebrow. Usually Lumination

had the longest lists on tour, never less than seven, especially for home shows.

Not wanting to pry, Bobo sat down the box and obliged, "Sí. I'll tell Ketchup. See you guys later." Bobo left, closing the door.

Amos launched up, flooded with frustration. He hissed through clenched teeth, "Mars, what were you *thinking?*"

"At least I wasn't in front of the door," Mars mocked.

Before Amos could reply, Dao pointed out, "Mars, Bobo could have *seen* that. Someone else could have came in through that open door—"

"I'm *fine,*" Mars interrupted. He turned and went to the door, "I'm going for a walk. No one follow me." He left, shutting the door.

Isaiah twirled a curl, "That is a ticking time bomb."

Amos rubbed his head, "It's like Mars don't even care!"

Dao shrugged, "He wants to be a monster, that's what."

"No," Amos defied, "Mars *thinks* he's a monster. I don't know what to say or do, though! Nothin' is gettin' through, dude!" he anguished.

The bassist summed up with a shrug, "Let him lay in his own bed, man. You did all that you could. I can take the press heat that will come from that. We all can. At least we won't have to hide Mars anymore."

Amos started toward the door, "I need to go after him."

Isaiah grabbed Amos' arm. The drummer tried to resist but Isaiah held firm as he said, "Let Mars *be.* He's a grown man, let him *be.* He's your cousin, not your child. Let Mars be Mars."

For the rest of the day, the remainder of Lumination Rising did not see Mars. Amos guessed he used his mind reading to evade them. Mars wasn't picking up his phone or answering texts, either.

The time was now eight-thirty, a half hour before Lumination Rising was to take the stage. Dao, Amos and Isaiah were in the dressing room getting dressed and ready for the show when Mars came in. He was already changed and with his wife and daughters behind him. They already had on their satin guest pass stickers, which looked identical to the all-access pass but without the glittering effect and they said "Guest" instead. The stickers were stuck to the Lumination Rising band shirts Danielle and the girls wore, all from the merch booth. The shirts were a little big for Vivica and Violet but nothing doused their brimming excitement.

Both Vivica and Violet blew into the room at the sight of Amos, who was tying his black sneakers. They screeched "Uncle Amos, Uncle Amos!" as they rushed to him.

Amos received them warmly and took them up in his arms. "Girls! Hey there!" The drummer gave each of them loving kisses on their heads as they hugged him. He tried to manage the girls as they climbed all over him, "Go say hi to Uncle Dao and Uncle Isaiah. Daddy, Mommy and I need to talk."

Immediately, the girls split up to climb all over Dao and Isaiah as Amos got up. The guitarist and bassist accepted the children gladly. Dao hefted Vivica in the air like an airplane and Isaiah wrapped Violet in an excited, playful hug.

To Mars and Danielle, Amos said, "Mi familia, uno momento, por favor." He walked past them and beckoned them to follow. Mars wanted to resist but Danielle took him by the hand and led.

Walking down the hall, Amos found an empty, unlocked room. They entered, Amos closed the door and flicked on the light.

Danielle asked, "What's going on?" A gentle anxiety brewed within her. She folded her arms, unsure of what to expect.

Amos shrugged and replied simply, "Mars goes on the bend a little. Just want to check in."

Mars assured, agitated, "I'm *fine*."

"I don't believe you," Amos accused. "Where were you all day?"

"'All day?'" Danielle echoed. "Mars? What happened? The girls and I just got here."

Mars replied gently to her, "I just had to clear my head, honey. First day jitters."

"Is the glass bothering you more?" Danielle asked, her voice marked with concern. She gently ran her hand along his forearm, it was smooth. She said to Amos, "I thought things were better." Improved mood, less random shards found around the house, Danielle sincerely thought Mars was on track to being his old self again.

"They *are*," Mars comforted.

Amos checked his phone, it was less than half an hour before showtime. He sucked his teeth, "Augh, we need to be on stage soon. Mars, you gotta pull it together and *keep it together* during our set. Dani, we're gonna have to link up after. Mars here isn't bein' entirely honest about how he's been–"

"Tell her now if you know," dared Mars, "I can tell it's running all over your *mind*."

"Mars, knock it off!" Amos admonished. "Stop doing that! Danielle, his abilities are more than glass. He can tell what I'm thinkin'."

"What?" Danielle was baffled. "He … what?"

Mars glowered at Amos but softened his face to Danielle when he said to her, "It's a little new but I can't hear everything. Just when it's about me, honey." He kissed her forehead. "I'm still learning it myself. I don't want to hear everything, though, so I try not to listen."

Danielle stood bolted to the spot. *Mars*, she thought, *I … can you hear me?*

Mars replied lovingly, "Yes, honey." He curled his hands around her wrists with gentle care, "Please, *please* don't be scared of me. Please don't run away." His heart sank at the words.

Amos tried to help as well. "Dani … Mars is … Mars is not a monster, I was shocked when I learned he could do this, too. But he and I, we've been working on it. Today's just been a little stressful." He hoped Danielle would take it well. Or at least in a way that wouldn't end with Mars going on a self-destructive warpath that would take the rest of San Diego with him.

Danielle thought, *Mars, my God. What did this explosion do to you? My ... please, Mars. If you can hear me, don't fight Amos. Please, I don't want you to go away again.* Danielle hugged Mars tightly. She said, "Please just do as I ask, honey." She didn't know how to take the news. The glass already was hard enough.

Mars rested his head upon hers and wrapped his arms around her. A small surge of jags crossed his back. He comforted, "I promise."

There was a quick knock on the door.

"Hey, anyone in here? Mars? Amos?" asked Ketchup, muffled through the door.

Mars called back, "We're in here."

Ketchup opened the door and poked his head in. "Hate to interrupt but everybody needs to be ready in ten. Dani, you and the girls are gonna be stage side on Isaiah's side. Anybody need anything?"

Everyone shook their head or said no.

"Okay," said Ketchup. "Have a good show." He closed the door.

Danielle kissed Mars on the chin, "Remember what I said, honey." To Amos, she said, "Keep Mars safe." As Danielle slid out of Mars' embrace, she felt some resistance. He was afraid to let her go. She pecked him on the cheek, patted his arm and left to go to the Lumination Rising dressing room.

Alone, together, Amos looked at Mars. He hoped Mars could keep it together, at least through their set.

"Cuz," said Amos, worn out, "let's try to have a good show."

Mars shrugged, lifeless. He wasn't prepared to face the crowd. But he had no choice.

As Amos and Mars walked out of the room, Cutie stood on stage in front of the cheering crowd. She wore a modded Dowry tour shirt herself, glinting gold spikes graced her thick, peach mahogany shoulders. Cutie wore ripped up black pants and heavy boots threaded with wide, gold laces that glittered in the spotlight. She was the only thing illuminated on stage, her shock red braids framed her plump face and wide, cherry gold smile. Though Cutie was short and stocky, she packed a lot of vivacious energy.

Cutie spoke into the beat up microphone with a squeaky, nasal voice as she addressed the crowd, "How is everyone doing!"

The crowd cheered jubilantly.

"We're home!" Cutie boasted. "First show of the Sugar and Spikes Tour! And you're all here! With us! To see us off, we thank you and love you all!"

The crowd cheered louder.

Cutie grinned with the mic at her side as the crowd went wild. Waves of glee and jubilation rippled through the packed venue. She returned the microphone to her lip and slowly announced, "Are you ready for Lumination Rising?"

Behind Cutie, a black and grey backdrop unfurled, revealing Lumination Rising's logo. The crowd raved.

Standing behind the stage, Mars felt the pressure building again. So many thoughts crowded his head. Amos collected Mars and brought him to the rest of the band waiting behind the curtain beside the stage.

Cutie giggled into the mic, "I will always love this part: Ladies and gentlemen! Girls and boys! Delirium Shack Records presents to you the first show of the Sugar and Spikes Tour! Everyone ... Lumination Rising!"

The lights went dark. Cutie placed the mic back in the stand and scurried off the stage as the crowd cheered.

When the show lights brightened, Dao and Isaiah stormed the stage, raring with energy. Amos hooked an arm around Mars' neck and they walked on stage together. Mars tried to smile through the buzz, though it was maddening. The crowd was thrilled, phones held up and bristling with baited anticipation. The screams swelled louder as the men got ready behind their instruments. Mars could barely register that he was in front of the microphone.

Each member had a simple print out of their set list taped to the floor. The first song was "Paper Chains", an old fan favorite. Amos led in with a bashing, staccato crash of his cymbals and the band began to play. The song was second nature to Mars, he threw himself into the lyrics and hoped it would distract him as he unhooked the microphone.

"I live my life, trapped in paper chains. Drowned in the inkwells, surrounded by the pain ...," he blared unsteadily to the roaring crowd.

Stage side, there stood Danielle and the girls. Both

Vivica and Violet wore neon protective headphones. Besides them stood Ketchup, Cutie and Savalez. Ketchup alternated between his tablet, his phone and the performance. Cutie swayed in place, following the song and mouthing the words. Savalez stood stoic, watching the show and audience with a calculative mind churning until Vivica and Violet ran up to him to dance. Bobo tried to watch the show but Mooch roped him at the start of the song to attend the merch table.

The show was immersive for Mars, it was like old times again. He thrashed about on stage, singing madly into the microphone without a care in the world. He didn't trip over the lyrics, the world felt normal. As they went into the second song, "Run Heartless", Mars' braid unfurled itself. Only Amos barely noticed as he banged away behind his silver drum-set in front of the banner. Vivica and Violet danced hand in hand with Savalez, the girls' backs turned to the stage. Danielle thought nothing of the unfurling, she was simply happy Mars appeared to be his old self again. The Mars she loved and married. Her heart swelled with confidence that everything was going to be fine; her husband, her family, their future.

Dao noticed Mars' dreads unfurling as he twirled his back towards the fans, strumming and slapping his ocean blue bass. He instinctively skipped forward to get beside Amos' drum-set and a thick amp. Isaiah spotted Mars' hair coming undone as well out the corner of his eyes as he riffed a fierce, fuzzy chord on his crimson guitar and sprang onto a tall speaker, using the smaller ones as steps.

Mars thrashed to and fro, wrapped up in himself. He had no idea a small spray of shards shook from his dreads during a low light moment and flung into the crowd. He just heard the screech of stranded guitar and felt himself rushed off stage. Panicked thoughts fluttered all around him, filling his head like sand. Most of them faded away as he was dragged to Lumination's dressing room by Isaiah.

Isaiah threw Mars into the room. Mars stumbled into the couch as Isaiah yelled, "No more! No more!"

Amos poured in after Isaiah while Dao kept his distance. Danielle tried to go past him but Dao clutched her wrist and pulled her back to be with Savalez and her daughters. Dao tried to calm her but she kept yanking her wrist and arguing back. Ketchup and Cutie were on stage doing crowd control and damage control. Their voices reverberated through the venue in English and Spanish, "Does anyone need help? Is everyone okay? Slight mishap, everyone!"

Furious, Amos raged, "Mars! You – you … we worked so *hard* on this! *You* worked so hard on this!"

Savalez swept past Dao and barreled in, swearing away in Spanish loudly. He got some hold on himself and bellowed in English, "Someone *explain!*"

Danielle snatched her wrist from Dao, he sighed and bundled up the girls, who grew upset in the turbulence.

"Girls first, then Mars," said Dao over the din.

Danielle's eyes burned red hot but Vivica's sharp wail made her set aside her anger and follow Dao to the empty room, away from the chaos. EMS and roadies rushed past them down the cinderblock hall.

In the dressing room, there stood Amos, flushed with broiling anger at Mars and hopelessness at Savalez. The room was quiet. Isaiah fumed as he stared at Mars, crumpled and cowering.

"EXPLAIN!" Savalez roared.

Mars drowned in the fury of Savalez's thoughts. Nothing but brute rage and terror, too awful for spoken words, thundered in Mars' head.

Next door, the members of The Dowry Effect heard the commotion through the wall. They gathered close together in the center of the room. Everyone hoped the wall could hold whatever Mars could throw at it. Their door ripped open, it was Cutie.

Cutie urged, "You're up. *Now.* Hurry! Hurry! Everything's ready!"

Lux asked, "How is Mar–"

"No time!" Cutie cut off. "Come on!"

The Dowry members filed out of the room quickly. They saw Savalez in a fury and Mars on the ground crumpled before him as they passed. Amos looked defeated, Isaiah was irate and flustered.

In Lumination's dressing room, Savalez approached Mars but Mars threw up a thick, jagged glass wall that curved over the couch.

"Stop! Yelling! At! Me!" Mars shouted as he clenched his head. He couldn't stand the thoughts any longer.

Savalez stumbled backwards in horror. "Diablo!" he gasped

"No!" Amos rebuffed. "He's not! This an effect from the

explosion he had. Still Mars!"

On stage, Deborah was on the microphone. The backdrop had already changed to that of The Dowry Effect, which was filled with pink and gold anarchist symbols among their logo. Their instruments, even Loco's gold drum-set, were ready. The crowd was muted and concerned. Only a few were still excited like before. The struck concert goers were already pulled out of the pit and laid in a cordoned off backstage area and checked over by medics. No fatal cuts, thankfully. Bits of glass still laid on the pit floor, crunched underfoot.

As Deborah wound the microphone around her forearm, she said into the mic, "Slight change in plans, folks. But the show must go on. The show must go on."

In Lumination's dressing room, Mars still had up his glass wall as Amos tried to reason with him.

"Mars," he begged, "put down the wall, please. Savale—"

The wall dropped down as Mars strained through the intruding thoughts, "This is me. This is me, now. Ever … ever since I left the hospital, all this time." A pillar of glass rose from the ground and propped up Mars to his feet before it lifted him off the floor from behind. He could hear Savalez's thoughts fade from anger and confusion into blank fear. Mars admitted with a dropped head, "This is me, now. Amos covered for me out of love. I messed up Dao's face by mistake. I control and make glass. I am this now."

Ketchup ran to Lumination's dressing room but stopped with a slide in the hall when he witnessed Mars rise. He darted to the door and slammed it shut behind him.

"Hi, Ketchup," Mars greeted darkly.

"Oh my God. Oh my God," Ketchup muttered over and over, propped up against the door. He traced a cross across his chest.

Amos urged, "Ketchup, calm down! This is an after effect of Mars' accident at the docks! Mars! Get down!"

"Why?" Mars asked, rolling his head back as more thoughts filled his mind like sand. His eyes were still on Ketchup and Savalez. "They won't fear me any less."

Isaiah begged, "Mars, *please!*"

His anger evaporated to steam, Savalez asked, "Is all this… true?"

Mars lowered himself and the pillar turned into a stool. He answered, "Every word." To Amos, Mars smirked, "So, how do you plan to spin this, cuz?"

It only took Amos a moment. "Savalez, Ketchup, please tell everyone a glass bottle broke – say someone threw a glass bottle!"

Both Savalez and Ketchup were taken aback. "What?" the both of them said.

"Please?" Amos agonized. "It's the only excuse we got. Or do you want the world knowin' 'bout Mars?"

Savalez pondered for a moment. He's seen a lot of outlandish things in his time in Rock music and plenty of crazy things as he grew up. But never, ever did he ever expect this. However, he knew Amos was right. The world couldn't know. The PR would be catastrophic, especially for a small, indie label. And with a new Lumination album coming out? The news about Mars could go south and get out of hand far too easily. Savalez didn't want to take such a chance. Already there were murmurs on Lumination's social feeds about Dao's face and how sliced up it looked from earlier that day.

Exasperated, Savalez turned to Ketchup and said in rapid Spanish, "Ketchup, after Dowry's set, end the night. Tell everyone there was a mishap with a glass bottle. Tell them we thought Mars was struck but he's fine. We're not canceling San Jose – yet. Tomorrow is supposed to be a travel day but we are staying tonight unless I say so. Keep Dowry out of this–"

Amos said in English, "The girls in Dowry already know about Mars. They helped us a little."

Savalez gritted his teeth and muttered in Spanish, "God save us." He continued to Ketchup, still in Spanish, "Let Dowry know we are having a meeting on Lumination's bus to decide what is *next*. There are several sold out shows, we can*not* cancel tour. *Not*."

The night ended early to Savalez's orders. The fans were disappointed but upon hearing the edited news about Mars, they begrudgingly understood. Some tried to linger but security cleared everyone out in minutes. Ketchup assisted as well. He wanted a little distance from Mars.

With the venue emptied, everyone piled onto Lumination's tour bus. Well, almost everyone – the techs and assistants were sent on their merry ways to load up the trailers for the next destination.

Danielle sat on the end of the long couch in the front of the bus, Vivica sound asleep on her lap. Violet slept on Isaiah's shoulder as he held her on his hip. He stood opposite of Danielle. Mars wanted to hold Violet but Isaiah made every excuse he could to prevent that. Defeated and depressed, Mars sat next to Danielle. He could tell she was hesitant of him holding Vivica as well. Headphones on and loud, his mind reeled with the thoughts of others.

Amos sat next to Mars. He could hardly find the right thing to say. "Everyone, this is … totally wild and crazy, I know."

Savalez sat across from Amos' side, flanked by Ketchup and Deborah on the short couch. Everyone wore bemused looks on their faces. Isaiah rolled his eyes.

"Understatement of the year," Loco said from the other end of the long couch. Amos glanced at her.

Lux and Nakia agreed from the small dining area. Dao nodded silently as he leaned against the kitchenette, arms crossed. His dreads laid against the right side of his face. He didn't dare want to check his phone, he already found a few comments about his face. He couldn't avoid it, they were mentions.

Deborah asked Savalez, "How are we gonna go forward? Is tour over?"

Savalez shook his head, "No, no, no, not at all."

Danielle leaned her head upon Mars' shoulder and held his hand. Mars squeezed her hand lovingly. Danielle squeezed back. *No matter what, Mars,* she thought solemnly,

I will always be by your side. He rubbed the back of her hand with his thumb.

Ketchup couldn't keep his eyes off Mars. He tried to hide his discomfort as he asked, "Mars, can you perform without... making, uh ... glass?"

Mars checked with his band members. Their faces were a range of concern and uncertainty. Amos and Isaiah worried that this was it for Lumination Rising. Mars couldn't blame them, the thoughts he heard on stage were deafening, it was hard to control himself. And when he thought getting lost in the music was better, tragedy struck. *I did it again,* Mars thought. *I hurt more people, innocent people.* His heart sank low. This was all on him.

"I ... I can wear tahms on stage if you need me to. They will hold whatever shard that–"

"Why weren't you wearing one tonight?" Savalez erupted. He calmed himself when Deborah, Danielle, Isaiah and Ketchup reminded him that there were sleeping children aboard.

Mars began to bristle a bit. His wife quelled him with a gentle squeeze of his hand. He reasoned, "I was doing better in practice so I thought I was fine."

Ketchup reported, "Five people got scratched up badly. One *might* need stitches."

Dao said, "Hopefully not."

Looking at Dao and his half covered face, Ketchup trailed off, "Yeah ... me, too." *Wow,* Ketchup thought, *Mars went to town on Dao, I still can't believe it. I hope nothing bad comes from this show. Those lawyers were not cheap with the*

Psychonauts and Chico always been stupid with women. We can't afford more cases. And Mars … he's … I hope nothing bad happens.

Savalez commanded, "Tahms from now on on-stage. No matter if it is a million degrees."

Mars nodded. He could live with that. Every time he glanced at Ketchup, Ketchup looked elsewhere. Mars could hear faint glimmers of words but the music drowned out the rest.

Savalez checked his phone. It was a bit past midnight. He looked at Vivica and Violet.

"The girls need to sleep," he said. "I'm sure they have school tomorrow."

Danielle and Mars nodded.

Savalez then commanded, "We're gonna switch Lumination and Dowry's set times for the rest of the tour. This way, a show won't get stopped so short and we have more prep time. I expect," Savalez looked at Amos, "I expect Lumination to be as normal as possible on the tour. We are *not* going to save Mars from every mishap. I *better* not hear anything frightening on the road." Amos nodded as Savalez looked at Mars to say firmly, "I also expect the men of Lumination to stay *safe*. Not a single *cut* or *nick*."

Mars nodded. He tried to absorb himself in the music as much as possible to prevent a short surge.

Savalez asked as he looked around the bus, "Any questions?"

Everyone said no or remained quiet.

"Very good," Savalez nodded.

The night was long and the Lumination Rising bus was quiet as it drove up the California state line to San Jose. The band and male tour crew slept sound in their beds, curtains drawn tight. Amos gave up his top bunk for the middle one under Mars', he was simply too drained to climb up. Top bunk empty and open, Amos was dead asleep in his middle bunk, curtain drawn tight.

Mars turned in his small bunk. The glass wall that lined behind his curtain was the only thing keeping him in his bunk as he tossed about. His jaw was tight, his brow furrowed. His mind was a torture chamber as bits of glass dripped from his skin and dreads.

He was back at the docks. The day was bright, humid and hazy with a dim yellow sky. He was back on the empty sidewalk down the old industrial side of town. His favorite place to walk when the pain of fame ever became too much. The day clapped loud with a riveting strike of thunder. He looked up and saw no clouds but shatters spread across the sky.

Mars looked at the aged brick wall of the chemical plant beside him. Fear and panic grasped him and he tried to run but his legs pumped too slow, like he was running through a bath of glue.

Behind him, he knew the bricks were breaking apart but slowly. He could sense and somewhat see in his head the rust brown bricks pull apart at the mortar seams. They were glacial in movement but he knew there was a dangerous force behind them. The sun grew hotter, it seared his skin with rage. He tried to shout for help, cry in anguish but he was silent. There was no one there. His skin started to bleed and melt – or so he felt but his body looked fine.

Mars tripped over his own feet, he couldn't breathe. His head full of fuzz, he had no idea he was on the ground until he could feel the grit against his cheek. The blast had yet to reach him visually but it already enveloped him through his other senses. He couldn't stop screaming in silence.

In the bunk beneath Mars, Amos began to stir from Mars' moving. Amos felt for his phone in the darkness beside his head and turned it on. The bunk glowed in a dim cast. It was just him, his pillow and the charger attached to his phone. He laid under a pale gold knitted sheet. Amos preferred his bunk uncluttered. Before Amos could open his eyes proper, a long shot of glass pierced the ceiling of his bunk. And another. And another.

The first spike scratched the pocket on the belly of his black hoodie. Amos was grateful he slept on his back. He sucked in his stomach to make for more space. The other, shorter spike pierced the ceiling by his ear and over his left hip.

With no time to think, the drummer swung his arm to break the longest shard and rolled out of his bunk. Amos landed on his socked feet as he rasped for air. He heard another javelin lance into his bunk as Mars thrashed in his sleep. Amos heard glances of panicked whimpers from Mars' bunk.

Amos ripped back Mars' curtain and faced the block of

glass. So dark and blurry, Amos could barely see his cousin. He dialed Mars, he didn't want to touch the glass. Amos hoped the plate wouldn't change into something worse.

Mars phone rattled and glowed against the plate as a jaunty, steel drum tune sang out. Amos half-hoped no one else would wake up but he also hoped they did so he could get them out.

The rattling of the phone near Mars' pillow made the vocalist flinch but the music woke him with a start. His heart was racing and there was broken glass in his mouth. Mars tried to swallow them but he coughed them out instead. His bunk was littered with shards and he felt several daggered in the bunk beneath him as the phone kept ringing. The world was dark and blurry outside his glass plate, only the phone gave any light.

Mars, pick up, Mars heard. He picked up the phone and answered, "What happened?"

Amos hissed, "Drop the glass block, you tried to *kill* me."

The partition fell. Amos saw a terrified Mars staring back at him. The cast of the phone luminated a sweating face, piercing eyes and a dropped, heaving jaw.

Amos hung up but kept his phone bright for light. He leaned himself into Mars' bunk and whispered, "Make *all* the glass disappear. All of it. Do you have any in your mouth?"

Mars opened his mouth wide for inspection. A few cavities and a couple silver fillings but nothing sharp glinted at Amos.

The drummer sighed, "Did you have another nightmare?"

Mars nodded. His breathing was ragged and heavy. His mind raced lightyears a second as his eyes danced about. Amos had seen this before. Especially during the first few nights when he kept Mars at his house.

"Try to calm down, okay?" Amos eased. "You ain't back there, alright? You're here. With everybody. Y'damn near got me like Dracula but I'm here."

Mars face twisted into a horrid frown. "Why does everyone keep me–"

"Uh-uh, holmes. None of that. It is far too late for that. We are gonna get some sleep and you gonna not be stabbin' family in your sleep," Amos said with tired certainty. He looked at Mars' phone. "You ain't have on that app I showed you? I thought it helped you sleep?"

Mars looked at his phone, it was dark. He tried to unlock the phone with a press of its button but it turned on instead. Then a low battery warning popped up and the phone died again. Craning his head, Amos saw the same.

"I think … I think the app drained the battery and cut itself off," Mars guessed. His voice was weak.

Amos rubbed his eyes and groaned, "Seriously? You don't charge your phone as you slee–"

Mars lifted his phone, the charging cord was crudely severed.

Amos rubbed his face. *Oh, come* on, *Mars,* floated across his mind.

"It wasn't on purpo–"

Amos halted his cousin, "I know, I know. But we gotta figure this out so you don't do this every night."

Mars suggested, "Maybe I could sleep in the back–"

"Nah, *no*," Amos waved off the thought, "You will get thrown about back there and we do not need a more moody Mars. We just gotta figure the tech out so you can sleep. You know what? I got the same charger as you. Gimme your phone, I'mma charge it. You still got your headphones?"

"They hurt my head when I wear them to sleep," Mars expressed.

"So have them *near* your head or above it until we get to the next spot as you sleep. I … wait … where's your speaker pillow?"

Mars motioned his head to his pillow. Lanced and slashed.

Amos sighed again. "I'm getting you another speaker pillow or *somethin'* because this gotta stop, *now*. You don't frost out when somethin' playin' next to you. At least not this bad." Amos looked over Mars' bunk and picked up his phone. "This will be with me. I'mma turn on the app, have your headphones ready, okay? It's gonna be a while before I'm sleepin' again–"

"I'm sorry, Am–"

"You're *fine*, man. That's why we're figurin' this out and keeping everything small." *So no one needs to know*, Amos thought. *You have to be old Mars as much as you can on this tour.*

Mars reached behind himself and pulled out his folded headphones. Little nicks graced the headband and the glass spikes on the ears were more intense but they still turned on.

"Glad *something* works," said Amos. "Alright, man. I'm plugging this up now, gimme a second." In his bunk, Amos unplugged his phone and hooked up Mars' instead. The screen flashed two percent and Amos turned it on. A quick boot up screen of brown and silver, then the home screen soon came to life. Displayed on the wallpaper was a sleeping lion on a stark white background. With a few scrolls and taps, classical foxtrot and ragtime over noises of a waterfall and birds sang out of Mars' headphones. It was an odd combination of sounds to Amos but whatever lulled Mars into a restful slumber, he kept and memorized. Because, if Mars could sleep peacefully, so could Amos.

Amos laid down Mars' phone, "Sounds like it's on." He went back to Mars' bunk.

Mars looked back at Amos, unsure. "Amos, are you ... will this be okay?"

"Haven't seen you frost this bad when this plays. It's my bunk so no one's gonna see the holes. We'll patch it up later and say we had too wild a party–"

"Y'think anyone gonna believe that?"

"If I'm the only one talkin', they will," Amos reassured. "Just try to chill and sleep, ok?"

Mars shifted himself onto his back, "I'll try."

"And don't spike your headphones, okay?" Amos warned.

Mars sighed and slid the headphones beside his head and raised the glass wall.

Night, Mars, Amos thought as he drew his cousin's curtain tight. He shook his head and looked at his bunk, roughly the size of a coffin and filled with holes. Amos decided to go to the front of the bus instead. Maybe watch some sports news on mute to soothe his head. *What a tour this will be,* he thought.

Epilogue

It was a hot day in Arizona. Everyone sat inside Club Alive by Sunrise, soaking up the air conditioning and enjoying all the club had to offer. As the roadies and crew set up the stage and pit, the bands enjoyed themselves. Deborah laid on a table mat in the tattoo parlor of the venue, she was getting a tattoo on her calf of a tumbling mass of vibrant peach blossoms. The rest of her band sat with Lumination Rising at the bar in the center of the club. They all were engrossed in a boxing match that played on the bar's many televisions. Senvi stood behind the bar, a tall, dark brown man with countless tattoos and a thick nose, co-owner of Club Alive by Sunrise. He mindlessly cleaned a glass cup as he watched the fight, leaned against the counter. He crouched down for a moment to check the volume, a bold Indian flag seated on the back of his neck just above the collar of his onyx shirt.

The club was large and lined with dark walls. Daylight shone bright through the large windows from the tattoo parlor section. Guitars hung everywhere, as were golden records, platinum records and framed pictures. The records were from B's band, Stacker St. The pictures spanned the history of the club but also the longer history of Stacker St., a six-piece alt-rock band that started almost a decade ago in Agoura Hills. Though everyone was from California, B was a Phoenix native. Every picture brimmed with life and mirth. One picture that stood over the bar was of the members of Stacker St. sitting on the bar. They were playing with colorful children instruments. Each of the men were as diverse as their sound, B only stood out with his wide brim black hat tilted on his head as he laughed wildly with a pair of maracas. The story behind the picture went that after the photo was taken, B fell off the bar and nearly took his drummer, Maverick, down with him. It was no secret that B was a bit accident prone. Both Lumination and Dowry saw that firsthand when they would tour together but it was always good times all around. Once, B darted down a concert hall with Chunks in tow. Dao chased after him but when he rounded a sharp corner, Dao discovered B toppled into a stack of packed boxes. Chunks was held up like a precious amulet, B landed flat on his back to prevent harm to Chunks. Though B received a light concussion, he still gave an outstanding show later that night.

At the far wall, there was a familiar face from the pictures. Andros Yamato wore a paint stained shirt and wielded a wide paint brush. His buzz cut hair was pastel lavender, his paint-splattered arms a milky brown. Yamato worked on a magnificent mural filled with street art, winged creatures and a few silly chibis thrown in. Cans of paint and spray cans surrounded him and stretched along the wall. Yamato barely missed the glass cup next to the spray cans. The area was a VIP sitting space but the musician claimed it for himself a few weeks ago, not long after B made his hasty departure. The unexpected departure canceled a tour, so Yamato took it upon himself to do this instead.

Yamato picked up the tall glass and focused on his recent color work. He looked down when he felt how light the glass was. It was empty, only the black straw remained. He placed down his paintbrush across a can of paint with speckled hands and brought his glass to the bar. Though he was neither very tall or very short, Yamato jumped over the white string partition he created weeks ago. He snagged his foot. Hopping on one foot, Yamato untangled himself and continued to the bar.

"Hey, Senvi!" Yamato said, his accent was a blend of Bolivian and Southern California that always stood out when he spoke. "Fill me up!" He grinned wide. Isaiah used to rib him about the juxtaposition of Yamato's accent and his last name. Then he wound up discovering it was indeed possible to be cursed out in Spanish and Japanese in the same sentence.

Senvi stared at Yamato and his held glass, astonished. He received the glass and remarked, "Andros, you are gonna drink B and I out of club and home." He filled the cup with seltzer water and readied the flavor pumps, "I'm about to cut you off of our Italian sodas and keep you on just tap water."

Yamato beamed a brighter smile. He charmed, "You know the band drinks free as long as we don't exhaust the bar. Besides, I designed at least three tats for B when we were a new band, it's clearing my balance sheet."

The two bands snickered at the exchange.

Seated beside Lux, Dao asked, "How is B doing, Yama?"

Yamato shrugged loosely as he received his refilled drink, "Still on radio silence. He *really* wanted a break. I text him everyday, though. The whole band does."

From afar, Deborah yelled ecstatically, "Andros Yamato! Ahhh, I haven't seen you in forever!" Flat gauze covered the back of her calf as she ran up to Yamato and tackled him with a hug.

"How goes it?" Yamato asked.

"Got a new tat!" Deborah gushed. She showed off the back of her calf as she stood on a single leg. "It's peach blossoms! How's everyone in Stacker, man?"

Yamato answered, "Everyone's good, B is still enjoying Bali."

Deborah laughed lightly, "Hopefully he'll be back soon. I miss his silly face."

Senvi rolled his eyes and said, "He'd better or this dude's gonna repaint this whole place."

Yamato replied to Senvi, "I'm givin' this place a makeover!" Yamato gestured to the building stage as he spoke to the bands, "You guys gonna be here tonight?"

Mars answered as he sat in front of an orange plastic cup filled with water, "Yep, that's us." Seated next to Amos, his dreads were drawn into a tight, low bun. It was an ultimatum from Ketchup over the heat and wearing a hat before showtime.

Yamato took a sip and said, "I hope you guys have a good show. I saw the video from the San Diego show last week. It looked *wild*, did Lumination get bottled?"

Amos answered quickly, "Yeah, it happens. The lights were low, too. Couldn't tell where it came from."

Yamato whistled. "Sucks, bro. Mars, it looked like it got you bad from how you got snatched from the stage. You alright?"

Mars answered with a smile and a passing chuckle, "I'm fine, I'm fine. It all worked out."

"That's good," Yamato said. "Dao! Are you doin' alright? I see you changed a bit since the last I saw you." He streaked a finger across the right side of his face, noting Dao's scars.

Dao uncomfortably laughed as he sat with a small crowd of chips and fries on a plate. He drank from a blue plastic cup. Besides the San Diego incident, his face was the talk among fans and onlookers at every stop of the tour so far. The attention jarred him a bit, especially the nit-picking kind. Sometimes he would not come out to meet fans at all, just wait for everyone to leave and briskly go from venue to bus. He couldn't stand the attention.

Dao replied, "I'm hangin' in there. My right eye is pretty much busted, though."

Mars heard Dao think, *Mars' handiwork. I wish people would stop asking about this for one day.*

Mars nudged Amos and muttered, "Dao doesn't wanna talk about the accident."

Amos chimed in quickly, "It's still a third rail for us, Yama. I'm sorry, holmes."

Yamato abruptly apologized, "Ah, I didn't mean to ... I'm sorry–"

Dao waved it off, "It's fine. Just don't mind me if I bump into stuff," he tried to joke. *Mars, you didn't have to tell Amos to save me ... But, thank you ... I guess,* Dao thought. He didn't know what to make of the save. He still had residual resentment towards Mars but he also noticed his many attempts to make up for what he did to him however he could. It was just that the constant talk about his eye made noticing Mars' goodwill attempts difficult. Very difficult, sometimes.

Mars looked at Dao. Dao continued focusing on Yamato. Mars looked away.

Yamato urged, "Get better, okay?" He stretched his arms above his head, Yamato had zero tattoos. Too terrified of needles. "I'm going to take a break. Have a good show tonight! I'll be watchin'." Yamato walked away, drinking his Italian soda through the thin straw.

Senvi uttered mostly to himself as he watched Yamato stroll away, "B better return soon. Andros is practically moving in. He even stumbled over something."

Deborah propped herself against the bar and remarked, "Ahhhhh, he just misses B a lot."

Senvi sucked his teeth and returned his attention to the television. "I suppose so. I miss B, too."

It was showtime and Dowry just finished their set. The crowd was ecstatic as Cutie and Ketchup watched stage side, out of view. The men of Lumination stood behind them. Mars wore a dark brown tahm with a cream stripe over his dreads, which were still in the bun, his headphones played droning techno to deal with the invading thoughts. He steadied himself with a hand on Amos' shoulder. The voices still fuzzed his mind and drowned his thoughts.

As Lux and Nakia gave lingering riffs, Deborah announced to the crowd, "Are. You. Ready!"

The crowd cheered loudly.

Deborah continued, speaking with a low-voiced pastor's fervor, "Are you ready ... for Lumination?"

The crowd screamed eagerly.

Loudly, Deborah announced slowly with a booted foot on the speaker, "Are you *ready* for Lumination Rising!" Both her pants legs were unfurled and normal.

The crowd went wild. Some started to chant "Lumination! Lumination! Lumination!" until it swelled into a deafening applause.

Quietly, Deborah spoke into the mic with her head bowed, "Get ready to receive illumination."

The lights went dim and the crowd roared. The members of The Dowry Effect left the stage to thundering applause and chants for the next band as well as theirs in alternation. They were patted on the back by Ketchup, Cutie and their fellow tour mates as they passed. Roadies ran by to assemble the new set as filler music played overhead.

Isaiah congratulated them, "Good show, good show."

Deborah grinned, "My leg hurts like hell right now. I'm gonna be laid out in the dressin' room."

Loco quipped behind Deborah, "Told ya, chica!"

Nakia suggested beside Loco, "Just prop your leg up and take some ibuprofen, you'll be fine."

Deborah said, "That sounds like an *amazing* idea. Gonna do that, now."

Lux tailed the group as they left the stage. She saw Mars' unsteady eyes and asked, "Mars, you think you gonna be alright?" He had done the last few shows to completion but his unfocused stares unsettled her sometimes. They even occasionally happened between songs. She guessed it was from the thoughts of fans and Amos almost never missed a chance to say that Mars was fine but still it concerned her and the rest of Dowry to not see Mars jumping around and hyped for the show like he used to.

Mars replied, a little distracted, "I think I'm getting a little better at this."

"That's good," Lux said. "Have a good show."

The women of The Dowry Effect and Cutie left, headed towards their dressing room in the well-lit hall of the club's backstage. The men of Lumination Rising stayed behind with Ketchup. The tour manager checked the text messages on his phone. "Bobo said it was a good thing he stayed with Mooch at the merch table," he said to Lumination over the filler music. "They are selling super well this tour!"

"That's good to hear!" Isaiah yelled back.

Mars!" Ketchup called out to the vocalist. He was still trying to adjust to Mars' reality. The most he told Bobo and

Cutie was that Mars was incredibly accident prone around glass so if they found shards around them, tell him *immediately.* Frankly, it was the best lie he could come up with because the truth still sounded batty to him. Though, Ketchup promised himself that he would share the truth by the end of the first leg of the tour. At Amos' recommendation, they kept a tighter line of communication.

Mars looked up, a little disoriented. The world around him was filled with deafening music and dizzying thoughts. He thought his legs would give out if he didn't hold on to Amos' shoulder.

"You ready, man?" Ketchup asked loudly.

Mars nodded, reading Ketchup's lips and hearing his thoughts. "I'm good," he called back.

Soon, it was Lumination's turn to hit the stage.

Each of the men assembled to the stage, one by one. Mars passed his headphones to Ketchup as he walked by. The thoughts were deafening again and the swirling lights didn't help. Mars tried to breathe steady and focus on his breath, just like Amos taught him. He unhooked the microphone and listened for Amos' cymbals. The set list by his feet stayed the same, Mars tried to focus on it as fans crowded the gates, yelling for his attention.

Once there was the staccato crash of cymbals, the show was on. Again, to bleed out the thoughts, Mars threw himself into the lyrics.

As the show went on, things improved bit by bit. Every show after San Diego had improved bit by bit. Mars always learned a new thing or two about his telepathy at every show, a new trick or insight to make it a bit more bearable. He learned to focus on the positive thoughts and bounce off them, it lessened the pressure in his head to something he could withstand.

As the show drew on into the final song, "Mercy Before Misery", Mars felt a bit more courageous. During a long guitar and drum bridge, Mars had an idea. As the riffs and beats built up into a swell, Mars backed up a step or two. At the climax, Mars darted out, off the ledge of the stage and onto a suspended plate of glass over the heads of amazed fans as he sung his part.

The rest of the band looked on with clueless wonderment. The roadies running to and fro behind the equipment stopped and stared. Ketchup panicked, he kept his eyes on the surging crowd. No one appeared hurt as the pit divided itself for a better look at Mars as he stretched out the plate halfway over the pit.

Mars could hear the surprise and glee of the fans around him. They thought it was a clever trick, something special for that particular show. His own band members were more alarmed. The roadies were confused, they wondered if they were supposed to know about the surprise. Ketchup wouldn't stop swearing, he thought Savalez would have Mars' head for sure. Mars turned on a booted heel and ran back onto the stage as the glass plate collected itself behind him into nothing. The band finished their final riffs and they ended their show.

"Thank you, Phoenix!" Isaiah announced to the cheering crowd as his band members left the stage.

Energized, Mars ripped off his tahm as he trotted from the stage. There were several shards inside.

As Mars passed Ketchup, the tour manager tailed him and boomed, "What was *that*? Mars! What *was* that!" He continued in Spanish, "Have you lost your *mind*?"

Mars kept strolling down the hall to the dressing rooms, focused on the thoughts of satisfied fans. He answered confidently, "I gave a good show. Everyone loved it!"

Amos ran ahead of Mars, stopping Mars in his tracks. Enraged, Amos blustered, "Mars, did you go *mad* again? What happ–"

"Dude!" Yamato cried at the sight of Mars. He sprinted up the hall, bouncing and darting between roadies. The red flannel shirt tied around his waist bobbed with every excited dodge and leap. Yamato clapped Amos' shoulders and shook them as he crowed, "That was so *sick*! What *was* that? It was like … oh, man! It was like being at a Bowie and Michael Jackson show all at once! That was *crazy*, man!" Yamato couldn't contain himself, he kept shaking Amos' shoulders.

Mars smiled earnestly, "Thanks, man."

Amos stood stunned and baffled, as did the other band members and Ketchup.

Think the story is over?

It isn't.

There's still music to be made

Dreams to be had

GLASS & DREAMS

Book 1 & 2

A Tie-In Duology between:

Dreamer

The Glassman

TBD 2026/2027

Other works

Null(Void)

In Search of Amika

Dreamer

Kinetics

About the Author

MultiMind lives in Baltimore, Maryland. She tries to find time for her countless hobbies, from 3D printing to bookbinding to virtual reality. She writes books that are fairly Black, usually queer, and very much embedded in the world of Sci-Fi, Fantasy & Horror.